TIME TO BE

Also by Eileen Campbell

A Dancing Star: Inspirations to Guide and Heal

TIME TO BE

REFLECTIONS ON

FACING THE FUTURE

EILEEN CAMPBELL

Thorsons

Thorsons

An Imprint of HarperCollins*Publishers*

77–85 Fulham Palace Road

Hammersmith, London W6 8JB

The Thorsons website address is: www.thorsons.com

Published by Thorsons 1999

1 3 5 7 9 10 8 6 4 2

A catalogue record for this book
is available from the British Library

ISBN 0 7225 3965 7

Printed in Great Britain by
Clays Ltd, St Ives plc

Contents

❧

Introduction

❧

TIME FOR A CHANGE

WE ARE LIVING THROUGH A PERIOD OF PROFOUND change, on both the personal and the collective levels. Whatever your view of the future, and the possible dawning of a new age, there is no doubt that now is an opportunity for new beginnings. Amidst the chaos of the present, there are many reasons for hope. We seem to be moving to a new level of awareness; we see new values in business, in medicine and science, even in government, trying to break through. There are tremendous forces for positive change, and many ideas once thought of only a couple of decades ago as fringe are now mainstream.

Now is the time to let go of the worn-out, the painful

and the sad, and to cross the threshold into a new era of promise. We need courage to let go, and to forgive the past. Whilst hopeful of new opportunities, we may be fearful of change – and so we need faith in something greater than ourselves. We need vision and inspiration to imagine a better future, not just for ourselves, but for each other and our children, and we wonder how we can make a difference.

Through the power of imagination we create the future. If we focus our thoughts and energy we have the capacity to influence the future. We have a choice. Just as we have created our present on one level (by our response to life's events), so we have a choice about the future we can create. What happens first in the mental realm manifests on the physical level. It is up to us. We need to take responsibility for our own health and well-being, play our part in our homes and workplaces, in the communities in which we reside, and in the wider global arena. The world is becoming ever-smaller as technology and transportation bring us closer together, and there is a growing realization that each one of us is linked to the whole. We may be poised, as some have argued, for our next evolutionary leap – a leap in consciousness. That leap involves a developing awareness, mindful and sustainable living, and allowing our inherent compassionate nature to emerge. To do that requires reflection, and time to be, something we all yearn for. It is in *being* that we connect with something greater than ourselves, and find both peace and the energy to sustain us in creating a world that works for all.

I hope that this anthology of inspirational quotations will be helpful in reflecting on those qualities we need in ourselves and our lives if we are to live fully in the present whilst creating our future.

It was the best of times,

it was the worst of times,

it was the age of wisdom,

it was the age of foolishness,

it was the epoch of belief;

it was the epoch of incredulity,

it was the season of light,

it was the season of Darkness,

it was the spring of hope,

it was the winter of despair.

CHARLES DICKENS (19TH CENTURY)

If mankind is not to perish after all the dread-
ful things it has done and gone through, then
a new spirit must emerge. And this new spirit
is coming not with a roar but with a quiet
birth, not with grand measures and words but
with an imperceptible change in the
atmosphere – a change in which each one
of us is participating ...

ALBERT SCHWEITZER (20TH CENTURY)

x

Wherever there is a withering of the law and
an uprising of lawlessness on all sides, *then* I
manifest myself.
For the salvation of the righteous and the
destruction of such as do evil, for the firm
establishing of the law, I come to birth age
after age.

Bhagavad Gita (2nd century bc – 2nd century ad)

The splitting of the atom has changed
everything save our mode of thinking, and
thus we drift toward unparalleled
catastrophe.

Albert Einstein (19th–20th century)

It may seem like a paradox, but one I think which will prove true, that only through directing ourselves toward the moral and the spiritual can we arrive at a state in which life on this earth is no longer threatened by some sort of 'megasuicide' and has a genuinely human dimension. This spiritual renewal is not something that one day will drop out of heaven into our laps, or be ushered in by a new Messiah. It is a task that confronts us all, every moment of our existence. We all can and must do something about it; we can't wait for anyone else.

VACLAV HAVEL (20TH CENTURY)

Who shall ascend into the hill of the Lord? Or who shall stand in this holy place? There is no one but us. There is no one to send, not a clean hand, nor a pure heart on the face of the earth, but only us, a generation comforting ourselves with the notion that we have come at an awkward time, that our innocent fathers are all dead – as if innocence has ever been – and our children busy and troubled, and we ourselves unfit, not yet ready, having each of us chosen wrongly, made a false start, failed, yielded to impulse and the tangled comforts of pleasures, and grown exhausted, unable to seek the thread, weak, and involved. But there is no one but us. There never has been.

ANNIE DILLARD (20TH CENTURY)

This world will change through you.

No other means can save it.

A COURSE IN MIRACLES (20TH CENTURY)

If humanity is entering a new world and a new consciousness, if a transformative shift is truly going on, then we must be awake to it and be part of it ... the fundamental nature of the transition is not the emergence of a new world but the emergence of a new spiritual and incarnational maturity. It is the emergence, not of new powers of awareness necessarily, but of new depths of responsibility, integrity, accountability and connectedness.

DAVID SPANGLER (20TH CENTURY)

Our myths and legends told us that we needed to preserve the old knowledge and keep it hidden so it would not be taken away or destroyed. We were told that a time would come when our knowledge and wisdom would be needed to save the planet, and that time is now. Now we must speak and share the wisdom of our ancestors.

ELDERS FROM HOPI, LAKOTA, CHEROKEE, MOHICAN, PAPAGO, MAORI, HAWAIIAN, SAMOAN, ABORIGINE, INUIT – NATIVE ELDERS THE WORLD OVER (20TH CENTURY)

Behold, I show you a mystery: We shall not all sleep, but we shall all be changed, in a moment, in the twinkling of an eye ...

1 CORINTHIANS 15: 51–2 (1ST CENTURY)

Humanity is learning a great lesson at this time. The lesson is, of course, to realize your godhood, your connectedness with Prime Creator and with all that exists. The lesson is to realize that *everything* is connected and that you are part of it all.

BARBARA MARCINIAK (20TH CENTURY)

All this world is heavy with the promise of greater things, and a day will come, one day in the unending succession of days, when beings who are now latent in our loins shall stand upon this earth as one stands upon a footstool and shall touch the stars.

H. G. WELLS (19TH–20TH CENTURY)

The new earth exists only in the heart
of man.

NIKOS KAZANTZAKIS (20TH CENTURY)

All nature is at the disposal of humankind. We
are to work with it. Without it we cannot survive.

HILDEGARD OF BINGEN (12TH CENTURY)

The ills from which we are suffering have their seat in the very foundation of human thought. But today something is happening to the whole structure of human consciousness. A fresh kind of life is starting.

PIERRE TEILHARD DE CHARDIN (20TH CENTURY)

The immediate prospect for fragmented Western man encountering the electric implosion within his own culture is his steady and rapid transformation into a complex person ... emotionally aware of his total interdependence with the rest of human society ...

Might not the current translation of our entire lives into the spiritual form of information make of the entire globe, and of the human family, a single consciousness?

MARSHALL MCLUHAN (20TH CENTURY)

Because we have acted with only partial awareness we
have upset the equilibrium and have torn the fabric of
the universe, which now returns to exact its ecological
reparation. Environmental degradation, alienation,
urban decay and social unrest are mirrors of the
shortness of our vision of man and the universe.
Our outer world reflects our inner conditions.

DUANE ELGIN (20TH CENTURY)

And what is the nature of the wasteland?
It is a land where everybody is living an
inauthentic life, doing as other people do,
doing as you're told, with no courage for
your own life.

JOSEPH CAMPBELL (20TH CENTURY)

You are the template, the prototype of a new and universal species, part solar, part material, both temporal and eternal, the species that will span the gulf between the visible and the invisible, bringing new worlds into form. Through you a new and unprecedented cycle of creation will occur.

KEN CAREY (20TH CENTURY)

The complexity of our time requires a greater and wiser use of our capacities, a rich playing of the instrument we have been given. The world can thrive only if we can grow. The possible society can become a reality only if we learn to be the possible humans we are meant to be.

JEAN HOUSTON (20TH CENTURY)

All will come again into its strength:

the fields undivided, the waters undammed,

the trees towering and the walls built low.

And in the valleys, people as strong

and varied as the land.

The houses welcoming all who knock

and a sense of boundless offering

in all relations, and in you and me.

No yearning for an afterlife, no looking beyond,

    no belittling death,

but only longing for what belongs to us

and serving earth, lest we remain unused.

RAINER MARIA RILKE
TRANSLATED BY ANITA BARROWS AND JOANNA MACY
(20TH CENTURY)

One

SEIZE THE DA
AND LIVE IN THE PRESENT
MOMENT

IN A WORLD OF EVER-ACCELERATING CHANGE, WITH urgent deadlines, shortened attention spans and short-term decision-making, time itself seems to have speeded up. We never have enough – we're 'time-squeezed'. We genuinely seem to have less than previous generations. Work no longer expands to fill the time available, but seems to spill over into our private lives. And even if we're not working, domestic life, in spite of labour-saving devices, seems increasingly hectic, as chores like shopping and taking the children to school or their leisure activities, have become ever more time-consuming. So we run faster and faster – impatient to get where, precisely? We live as though we are although death is never far away! In our rush to live, we miss the very things which keep us grounded and bring balance to our lives. Somehow we have lost the plot, and before we know it another year will have zoomed by, it will be months since we last saw our parents, our relationships seem fraught, our health isn't great, and there's a deep-down feeling that there must be more to life than this frenetic activity and struggling to find our way through the overwhelming deluge of confusing information that bombards us from all directions. For that seems to be a penalty of progress. Sifting information in order to make choices now devours an increasing amount of time.

We need to stop, slow down and say no to the insanity. We need to breathe! We need a more reflective and contemplative approach to life. Being, as opposed to doing, means letting things be as they are, not trying to fix them, but letting everything unfold in its own way. It's a more feminine mode, one which is receptive, holistic, intuitive, rather than a masculine mode which is dynamic, rational and logical. We need both modes, but they need to be in balance. When we restore balance to our lives and turn our backs on the instant gratification that our society seems to expect of us, we can choose to create a more joyful way of living. To do that, we need to live in the present moment. That means accepting it as it is, without imposing anything else on it or trying to change it, and letting it unfold to the next moment.

The problem is, we rarely live in the present moment. All too often we are living in the past, preoccupied with something that has happened to us; or we are living in the future, waiting for a time when life will treat us magnificently and we will be happy; or worrying about what lies ahead and how we will cope. Or we may just be putting off all those things we promised ourselves we would do when we have time. But, every day of our lives brings the opportunity for a new beginning and there was never a better time to be.

Shortage of time is the greatest shortage
of our time.

FRED POLAK (20TH CENTURY)

The butterfly counts not months but
moments and has time enough.

RABINDRANATH TAGORE (19TH–20TH CENTURY)

Caretake this moment.

Immerse yourself in its particulars. Respond
to this person, this challenge, this deed.

Quit the evasions. Stop giving yourself needless
trouble.

It is time to really live; to fully inhabit the situation you happen to be in now.

EPICTETUS (1ST–2ND CENTURY)

4

The more a person is able to direct his life consciously, the more he can use time for constructive benefits. The more, however, he is conformist, unfree, undifferentiated, the more, that is, he works not by choice but by compulsion, the more he is then the object of quantitative time ... The less alive a person is – 'alive' here defined as having conscious direction of his life – the more is time for him the time of the clock. The more alive he is, the more he lives by qualitative time.

ROLLO MAY (20TH CENTURY)

Eternity is not the hereafter. Eternity has nothing to do with time ... This is it. If you don't get it here, you won't get it anywhere. The experience of eternity right here and now is the function of life. Heaven is not the place to have the experience; here's the place to have the experience.

JOSEPH CAMPBELL (20TH CENTURY)

For if we open our eyes and see clearly, it becomes obvious that there is no other time than this instant, and that the past and the future are abstractions without any concrete reality. Until this has become clear, it seems that our life is all past and future, and that the present is nothing more than the infinitesimal hairline which divides them. From this comes the sensation of 'having no time', of a world which hurries by so rapidly that it is gone before we can enjoy it. But through 'awakening to the instant' one sees that this is the reverse of the truth: it is rather the past and future which are the fleeting illusions, and the present which is eternally real.

ALAN WATTS (20TH CENTURY)

This existence of ours is as transient as autumn
   clouds.
To watch the birth and death of beings is like look-
   ing at the movements of a dance.
A lifetime is like a flash of lightning in the sky,
Rushing by, like a torrent down a steep mountain.

THE BUDDHA (6TH CENTURY BC)

It's only when we truly know and understand
that we have a limited time on earth – and that
we have no way of knowing when our time is
up – that we will begin to love each day to the
fullest, as if it was the only one we had.

ELIZABETH KÜBLER ROSS (20TH CENTURY)

If I could only remember that the days
were not bricks to be laid row on row, to be
built into a solid house, where one might
dwell in safety and peace, but only food for
the fires of the heart.

EDMUND WILSON (20TH CENTURY)

Time is what keeps the light from reaching
us. There is no greater obstacle to God
than time.

MEISTER ECKHART (13TH–14TH CENTURY)

When there is no desire to satisfy yourself,
there is no aggression or speed ... Because
there is no rush to achieve, you can afford
to relax, you can afford to keep company
with yourself.

CHÖGYAM TRUNGPA (20TH CENTURY)

As long as we have some definite idea
about or some hope in the future, we cannot
really be serious with the moment that
exists right now.

SHUNRYU SUZUKI-ROSHI (20TH CENTURY)

Your future has nothing to do with getting
somewhere you think you need to be. It has
to do with the awareness that getting *there*
means *being* here.

CARL A. HAMMERSCHLAG (20TH CENTURY)

If the world stands bewildered and confused
in the face of its trouble, it is partly because
we Westerners have made a god of activity;
we have yet to learn how to be, as we have
already learnt how to do.

PAUL BRUNTON (20TH CENTURY)

And the days are not full enough
And the nights are not full enough,
And life slips by like a fieldmouse
Not shaking the grass.

EZRA POUND (20TH CENTURY)

Gather ye rosebuds while ye may,
Old Time is still a-flying:
And this same flower that smiles to-day,
To-morrow will be dying.

ROBERT HERRICK (17TH CENTURY)

The future is made of the same stuff as
the present.

SIMONE WEIL (20TH CENTURY)

I meant to do my work today,

But a brown bird sang in the apple tree,

And a butterfly flitted across the field,

And all the leaves were calling me.

And the wind went sighing over the land.

Tossing the grasses to and fro,

And a rainbow held out its shining hand –

So what could I do but laugh and go?

RICHARD LE GALLIENNE (19TH–20TH CENTURY)

To affect the quality of the day, that is the
highest of the arts.

HENRY DAVID THOREAU (19TH CENTURY)

No mind is much employed upon the
present; recollection and anticipation fill
up almost all our moments.

SAMUEL JOHNSON (18TH CENTURY)

You would measure time the measureless and the
   immeasurable.
You would adjust your conduct and even direct the
   course of your spirit according to the hours
   and seasons.
Of time you would make a stream upon whose
   bank you would sit and watch its flowing.

Yet the timeless in you is aware of life's
   timelessness,
And knows that yesterday is but today's memory
   and tomorrow is today's dream.
And that which sings and contemplates in you is
   still dwelling within the bounds of that first
   moment which scattered the stars into space.

KAHLIL GIBRAN (20TH CENTURY)

Ah, fill the Cup: – what boots it to repeat
How Time is slipping underneath our Feet.

EDWARD FITZGERALD (19TH CENTURY)

Some there are that torment themselves
afresh with the memory of what is past;
others, again, afflict themselves with the
apprehension of evils to come; and very
ridiculously – for the one does not now con-
cern us, and the other not yet ... One should
count each day a separate life.

SENECA (1ST CENTURY BC)

But at my back I always hear
Time's wingèd chariot hurrying near,
And yonder all before us lie
Deserts of vast eternity.

ANDREW MARVELL (17TH CENTURY)

Everything flows on and on like this river,
whithout pause, day and night.

CONFUCIUS, ANALECTS (6TH CENTURY BC)

Was then not all sorrow in time, all self-
torment and fear in time? Were not all
difficulties and evil in the world conquered
as soon as one conquered time, as soon
as one dispelled time?

HERMANN HESSE (20TH CENTURY)

Be watchful of time and how you spend it.
Nothing is more precious than time. In the
twinkling of an eye heaven may be won
or lost.

CLOUD OF UNKNOWING (14TH CENTURY)

The time of life is short!
To spend that shortness basely were too long.

WILLIAM SHAKESPEARE
HENRY IV PART I, ACT V.II (16TH CENTURY)

Time is but the stream I go a-fishing in.

H. D. THOREAU (19TH CENTURY)

Slow me down, Lord!

Ease the pounding of my heart by the quieting of
my mind.

Steady my hurried pace with a vision of the
Eternal reach of time.

Give me, amidst the confusion of my day, the
calmness of the Everlasting hills.

Break the tensions of my nerves and muscles with
the soothing music of singing streams that live
in my memory.

Help me to know the magical restoring power of
sleep.

Teach me the art of taking minute vacations ... of
slowing down to look at a flower, to chat with
a friend, to pat a dog, to read a few lines from
a good book.

Remind me each day of the fable of the hare and
the tortoise, that I may know that the race is
not always to the swift; that there is more to
life than measuring its speed.

Let me look upwards into the branches of the
 towering oak, and know that it grew great and
 strong because it grew slowly and well.
Slow me down, Lord, and inspire me to send my
 roots deep into the soil of life's enduring
 values that I may grow towards the stars of my
 enduring destiny.

(FROM *LOVE IS MY MEANING*, EDITED BY E. BASSETT)
(20TH CENTURY)

It is most important that we learn to practise Full Awareness of Breathing during our daily lives. Usually, when we perform our tasks, our thoughts wander, and our joys, sorrows, anger, and unease follow close behind. Although we are alive, we are not able to bring our minds into the present moment, and we live in forgetfulness.

We can begin by becoming aware of our breath, by following our breathing. Breathing in and breathing out, we know we are breathing in and out, and we can smile to affirm that we are ourselves, that we are in control of ourselves. Through awareness of breathing, we can be awake in and to the present moment.

THICH NHAT HANH (20TH CENTURY)

Days are made of moments.

All are worth exploring.

Many kinds of moments,

None is worth ignoring.

All we have are moments ...

STEPHEN SONDHEIM (20TH CENTURY)

Adopt the pace of nature,

her secret is patience.

RALPH WALDO EMERSON (19TH CENTURY)

Our inner lives are timeless,

and yet our days are numbered.

GUNILLA NORRIS (20TH CENTURY)

There is only one time when it is essential
to awaken. That time is now.

THE BUDDHA (6TH CENTURY BC)

We join spokes together in a wheel,
but it is the center hole
that makes the wagon move.

We shape clay into a pot,
but it is the emptiness inside
that holds whatever we want.

We hammer wood for a house,
but it is the inner space
that makes it liveable.

We work with being,
but non-being is what we use.

LAO TZU (4TH CENTURY BC)
TRANSLATED BY STEPHEN MITCHELL

Two

∿

IMAGINE THE FUTURE —
FOLLOW YOUR DREAM

IMAGINATION IS A POWERFUL TOOL – WHAT WE CAN imagine we can create. If we can create a vision on the mental level we can bring that through on the material level, with dedication and application. 'Where there is no vision the people perish', says the Old Testament, and in facing the future, a vision is vital. In our darkest moments it is the vision which spurs us on. We need to use our imagination to picture new ways of being. We need a dream that is our very own, which springs from who we really are and what we truly value. If it comes from the depths of our being it will be what we really want and need. We must then hold on to this dream – the vision has to be honoured every day of our lives. Making imagination our ally, we can work with positive images to give our dreams direction, for by being optimistic we give our vision energy. In that process of holding on to the dream, it's as if we enlist the support of the universe and countless hands reach out to guide us. Opportunities arise, doors open, and all kinds of assistance seems to appear as if from nowhere.

But what if we don't know exactly what it is we want for the future. How do we access vision, or retain it? Dreaming is part of being human, and when we pursue our dreams, new energy is available to us. We need to give ourselves time; if we take the time to listen then we can connect with a higher power, the source of all creativity. Inspiration will flood in to fuel the imagination, the mists will clear and gradually, as we allow the inspiration to work on us, we will begin to see what it is we truly want for the future. When that vision comes from the deepest part of ourselves and is of something more peaceful, more fulfilling, more loving, if we focus our minds on it, then there is no doubt whatsoever that we will be able to bring that future into being.

I am certain of nothing but of the holiness of
the heart's affections, and the truth of the
Imagination.

JOHN KEATS, LETTER 20TH NOVEMBER 1817

It is the imagination that gives shape to
the universe.

BARRY LOPEZ (20TH CENTURY)

This world of Imagination is the world of
Eternity. It is the bosom into which we shall
go after death of the vegetated body. This
world of Imagination is Infinite and Eternal,
whereas the world of generation is finite and
temporal. All things are comprehended in
their Eternal Forms in the divine body of
the Saviour, the true voice of Eternity, the
Human Imagination.

WILLIAM BLAKE (18TH–19TH CENTURY)

The world of reality has its limits. The
world of imagination is boundless.

JEAN-JACQUES ROUSSEAU (18TH CENTURY)

If one advances confidently in the direction
of his dreams and endeavors to live the life
which he has imagined, he will meet with a
success unexpected in common hours.

HENRY DAVID THOREAU (19TH CENTURY)

If you follow your bliss, you put yourself on
a kind of track, which has been there all the
while, waiting for you, and the life that you
ought to be living is the one you are living.

JOSEPH CAMPBELL (20TH CENTURY)

Vision brings new appreciation of what there is. It makes a person see things differently, rather than see different things. After all, nobody can ever escape Being, least of all his own being. It is the vision that gives meaning to our experiences and our actions by making us face the problem, and therefore also vision alone gives man a sense of direction and enables him to sketch a map which will guide him in his task of finding himself rather than running away from himself.

HERBERT GUENTHER (20TH CENTURY)

What you can do, or dream you can – begin it. Boldness has genius, power and magic in it.

JOHANN WOLFGANG GOETHE (18TH CENTURY)

Your life proceeds out of your intentions for it.

NEALE DONALD WALSCH (20TH CENTURY)

When you are inspired by some great purpose, some extraordinary project, all your thoughts break their bonds; your mind transcends limitations, your consciousness expands in every direction, and you find yourself in a new, great and wonderful world. Dormant forces, faculties and talents become alive, and you discover yourself to be a greater person by far than you ever dreamed yourself to be.

PATANJALI (2ND CENTURY BC)

Imagination is more than knowledge.

ALBERT EINSTEIN (20TH CENTURY)

Our aspirations are our possibilities.

ROBERT BROWNING (19TH CENTURY)

Before you begin a thing, remind yourself that difficulties and delays quite impossible to foresee are ahead. If you could see them clearly, naturally you would do a great deal to get rid of them but you can't. You can only see one thing clearly and that is your goal. Form a mental vision of that and cling to it through thick and thin.

KATHLEEN NORRIS (20TH CENTURY)

The real voyage of discovery consists not in seeking new landscapes, but in having new eyes.

MARCEL PROUST (19TH–20TH CENTURY)

Vision is the capacity to believe in what my heart sees, what others can't see. Vision is seeing positive possibilities where others see only negative probabilities.

CARL A. HAMMERSCHLAG (20TH CENTURY)

And I have the firm belief in this now, not only in terms of my own experience but in knowing about the experience of others, that when you follow your bliss, doors will open where you would not have thought there were going to be doors and where there wouldn't be a door for anybody else.

JOSEPH CAMPBELL (20TH CENTURY)

Some men see things as they are and ask, 'Why?'
I dream things that never were and ask, 'Why not?'

GEORGE BERNARD SHAW (19TH–20TH CENTURY)

If you have built castles in the air,

your work need not be lost;

that is where they should be.

Now put foundations under them.

HENRY DAVID THOREAU (19TH CENTURY)

This, I thought, is how great visionaries and

poets see everything – as if for the first time.

Each morning they see a new world before

their eyes; they do not really see it, they

create it.

NIKOS KAZANTZAKIS (20TH CENTURY)

Ideals are like stars: you will not succeed in touching them with your hands. But like the seafaring man on the desert waters, you choose them as your guides, and, following them you will reach your destiny.

CARL SCHURZ (19TH CENTURY)

May the vision that so many mystic masters of all traditions have had, of a future world free of cruelty and horror, where humanity can live in the ultimate happiness of the nature of mind, come, through all our efforts, to be realized.

SOGYAL RINPOCHE (20TH CENTURY)

You are never given a wish without also being given the power to make it true. You may have to work for it, however.

RICHARD BACH (20TH CENTURY)

The eye by which I see God is the same eye
by which God sees me.

MEISTER ECKHART (13TH CENTURY)

While with an eye made quiet by the power
of harmony, and the deep power of joy, we
see into the life of things.

WILLIAM WORDSWORTH (19TH CENTURY)

Because you cannot see me with your own
natural eye, I will give you a celestial eye.

BHAGAVAD GITA (2ND CENTURY BC–2ND CENTURY AD)

Progress will be carried forward by a series
of dazzling visions.

VICTOR HUGO (19TH CENTURY)

❧

The heart is nothing but the Sea of Light,
the place of vision is God.

JALAL AL-DIN RUMI (13TH CENTURY)

❧

And so there comes a time – I believe we are in such
a time – when civilization has to be reviewed by the
discovery of new mysteries, by the undemocratic but
sovereign power of the imagination ... the power that
makes all things new.

NORMAN O. BROWN (20TH CENTURY)

❧

The future is not there waiting for us.
We create it by the power of imagination.

PIR VILAYAT KHAN (20TH CENTURY)

Three

❧

FEAR IS AN ILLUSION – DARE TO BE YOURSELF

FEAR IS A NATURAL RESPONSE TO DANGER, WHEN OUR survival is threatened, but all too often we are afraid unnecessarily. We may be afraid of making mistakes, of trying something new or of confrontation. We may fear poverty, ill-health, or old age. But fear in these circumstances is paralyzing – it closes down the heart and distorts our perception. As a result, our lives narrow down, we take fewer risks, and get stuck in our habitual grooves, preferring to stay in our familiar comfort zones. In doing that we fail to fulfil our real potential as human beings and in extreme cases we fail even to live, but instead stagnate until we are dead inside.

Underlying all fear is the failure to understand that we are not separate from the source of life. Once we see that, then we can let go of fear and learn to live only in the present moment. Fear is an illusion. We need to release the potential energy locked up in fear, to enable us to live our lives fully. To do that we need to be courageous, and act 'as if' we are unafraid. Easier said than done, of course, but we need to practise being brave. The more we are prepared to fight on, face to face with our fear, the more likely we are to triumph.

You gain strength and courage and
confidence by every experience in which
you really stop to look fear in the face.

ELEANOR ROOSEVELT (20TH CENTURY)

It is not because things are difficult that
we do not dare; it is because we do not
dare that they are difficult.

SENECA (1ST CENTURY)

... courage is not the absence of despair; it is,
rather the capacity to move ahead *in spite
of despair*.

ROLLO MAY (20TH CENTURY)

There is a tide in the affairs of men,

Which, taken at the flood, leads on to fortune;

Omitted, all the voyage of their life

Is bound in shallows and in miseries.

On such a full sea are we now afloat;

And we must take the current when it serves,

Or lose our ventures.

WILLIAM SHAKESPEARE
JULIUS CAESAR IV:III (16TH CENTURY)

To reach the port of Heaven,

we must sail sometimes with the wind,

sometimes against it,

but we must sail and not drift or lie at anchor.

OLIVER WENDELL HOLMES (19TH CENTURY)

Who dares nothing, need hope for nothing.

FRIEDRICH VON SCHILLER (18TH CENTURY)

'Come to the edge.' 'No, we will fall.'
'Come to the edge.' 'No, we will fall.'
He came to the edge. They pushed him, and he
flew.

GUILLAUME APOLLINAIRE (20TH CENTURY)

Fear not that thy life shall come to an end,
but rather fear that it shall never have a
beginning.

CARDINAL NEWMAN (19TH CENTURY)

Life shrinks or expands according to one's
courage.

ANAÏS NIN (20TH CENTURY)

Let me not pray to be sheltered from the dangers,
but to be fearless in facing them.
Let me not beg for the stilling of my pain,
but for the heart to conquer it.
Let me not look for allies in life's battlefield,
but to my own strength.
Let me not crave in anxious fear to be saved,
but hope for the patience to win my freedom.

RABINDRANATH TAGORE (19TH–20TH CENTURY)

To have courage for whatever comes in life –
everything lies in that.

SAINT TERESA OF AVILA (16TH CENTURY)

Life only demands from you the strength you
possess.
Only one feat is possible – not to have run away.

DAG HAMMARSKJÖLD (20TH CENTURY)

Each man has inside him a basic decency and goodness. If he listens to it and acts on it, he is giving a great deal of what it is the world needs most. It is not complicated, but it takes courage for a man to listen to his own inner goodness and act on it. Do we dare to be ourselves? This is the question that counts.

PABLO CASALS (20TH CENTURY)

The human heart can go the lengths of God.

Dark and cold we may be, but this

Is no winter now. The frozen misery

Of centuries breaks, cracks, begins to move;

The thunder is the thunder of the floes,

The thaw, the flood, the upstart Spring.

Thank God our time is now when wrong

Comes up to face us everywhere,

Never to leave us till we take

The longest stride of soul men ever took.

Affairs are now soul size.

The enterprise

Is exploration into God.

Where are you making for? It takes

So many thousand years to wake

But will you wake for pity's sake?

CHRISTOPHER FRY (20TH CENTURY)

A great deal of talent is lost to the world for want of a little courage. Every day sends to their graves obscure men whom timidity prevented from making a first effort.

SYDNEY SMITH (19TH CENTURY)

Heroes take journeys, confront dragons, and discover the treasure of their true selves. Although they may feel very alone during the quest, at its end their reward is a sense of community: with themselves, with other people, and with the earth. Every time we confront death-in-life we confront a dragon, and every time we choose life over nonlife ... we vanquish the dragon; we bring new life to ourselves and to our culture.

CAROL PEARSON (20TH CENTURY)

Four

MASTER YOUR MIND —
YOU ARE WHAT YOU THINK

WE HAVE A CHOICE WHEN WE CONSIDER THE FUTURE.
It is within our power to create a positive one, or we can
stare into the abyss and be fearful. What we give energy to
by thinking about and believing becomes reality. Our
thoughts ultimately give rise to the very thing they envis-
age, so we have the capacity to make ourselves happy and
be at peace, just as much as to be sad, angry and depressed.
And the average human being is supposed to have 60,000
thoughts in a single day!

Though we may not be able to prevent what happens
to us in the first place, it is within our capability to determine our reaction to an event, and look at it from a different

perspective. An illness, a disappointment or a betrayal can be devastating, but it is also an opportunity to learn and to understand. It may not seem so at first, but gradually, as we take the time to reflect on what has happened, we begin to shift our perspective, and the pain eases.

In the mental realm, like attracts like, and so it is important to focus on inspiring and positive thoughts. As we do that, we are choosing our future. It's not easy of course, but if the will and intention are strong, and if we surround ourselves with those things which inspire us, whether a beautiful piece of music, a picture, a flower ... then with time and patience, we begin to make progress.

Working to change our thought patterns will determine the kind of world we live in. In this way we exercise our free will, so that whatever our circumstances we can help to create a peaceful and loving world, if we so choose.

No great improvements in the lot of
mankind are possible, until a great change
takes place in the fundamental constitution
of their modes of thought.

J. S. MILL (19TH CENTURY)

Every thought you have makes up some
segment of the world you see. It is with your
thoughts, then, that we must work, if your
perception of the world is to be changed.

A COURSE IN MIRACLES (20TH CENTURY)

As a man thinks, so does he become.
Every man is the son of his works.

CERVANTES (16TH CENTURY)

It lies within ourselves or our own actions

To possess happiness;

Or by sloth and negligence

To fall from happiness into ruin.

ORIGEN (3RD CENTURY)

You create your reality according to your beliefs.

Yours is the creative energy that makes your world.

JANE ROBERTS (20TH CENTURY)

Great men are they who see that the

spiritual is stronger than any material force;

that thoughts rule the world.

RALPH WALDO EMERSON (19TH CENTURY)

Our life is what our thoughts make it.

MARCUS AURELIUS (2ND CENTURY)

All that we are is the result of what we have thought: all that we are is founded on our thoughts and formed of our thoughts. If a man speaks or acts with an evil thought, pain pursues him, as the wheel of the wagon follows the hoof of the ox that draws it.

All that we are is the result of what we have thought: all that we are is founded on our thoughts and formed of our thoughts. If a man speaks or acts with a pure thought, happiness pursues him like his own shadow that never leaves him.

THE DHAMMAPADA (6TH CENTURY BC)

You must be the change you want to see
in the world.

M. K. GANDHI (20TH CENTURY)

The world is a looking glass and gives back
to every man the reflection of his own face.

WILLIAM MAKEPEACE THACKERAY (19TH CENTURY)

We have it in our power to begin the world
again.

THOMAS PAINE (18TH CENTURY)

... everything can be taken away from a man
but one thing: the last of human freedoms –
to choose one's attitude in any given set of
circumstances, to choose one's own way.

VIKTOR FRANKL (20TH CENTURY)

Even as radio waves are picked up
whenever a set is tuned in to their
wavelength, so the thoughts which each of
us think each moment of the day go forth
into the world to influence for good or bad
each other human mind.

CHRISTMAS HUMPHREYS (20TH CENTURY)

Peace of mind is clearly an internal matter. It must begin with your own thoughts, and then extend outward.

It is from your own peace of mind that a peaceful perception of the world arises.

A COURSE IN MIRACLES (20TH CENTURY)

When a little bubble of joy appears in your
sea of consciousness, take hold of it and
keep expanding it. Meditate on it and it will
grow larger. Keep puffing at the bubble
until it breaks its confining walls and
becomes a sea of joy.

PARAMAHANSA YOGANANDA (20TH CENTURY)

We must steadfastly practise peace, imagining
our minds as a lake ever to be kept calm, without waves, or even ripples, to disturb its tranquility, and gradually develop this state of
peace until no event of life, no circumstance,
no other personality is able under any condition to ruffle the surface of that lake or raise
within us any feelings of irritability, depression
or doubt ... and though at first it may seem to
be beyond our dreams, it is in reality, with
patience and perseverance, within the reach of
us all.

DR. EDWARD BACH (20TH CENTURY)

Happiness and freedom begin with a clear understanding of one principle: some things are within your control, and some things are not. It is only after you have faced up to this fundamental role and learned to distinguish between what you can and can't control that inner tranquility and outer effectiveness become possible.

EPICTETUS (1ST–2ND CENTURY)

You have the power to heal your life, and you need to know that. We think so often that we are helpless, but we're not. We always have the power of our minds ... Claim and consciously use your power.

LOUISE L. HAY (20TH CENTURY)

The greatest revolution in our generation
is the discovery that human beings,
by changing the inner attitudes of their minds,
can change the outer aspects of their lives.

WILLIAM JAMES (19TH CENTURY)

The mind is its own place, and in itself
Can make a heaven of Hell, or a hell of Heaven.

JOHN MILTON (17TH CENTURY)

'I can't believe that,' said Alice.

'Can't you?' the Queen said, in a pitying tone.

'Try again: draw a long deep breath and shut your eyes.'

Alice laughed, 'There's no use trying,' she said. 'One can't believe impossible things.'

'I dare say you haven't had much practice,' said the Queen. 'When I was younger, I always did it for half an hour a day. Why, sometimes I've believed in as many as six impossible things before breakfast.'

LEWIS CARROLL (19TH CENTURY)

Most people think that external life will
give them what they crave and seek ... Life
comes in as impressions and it is here that it
is possible to *work on oneself* ... No one can
transform external life. But everyone can
transform his impressions.

MAURICE NICOLL (20TH CENTURY)

Whatsoever things are true,
whatsoever things are honest,
whatsoever things are just,
whatsoever things are pure,
whatsoever things are lovely,
whatsoever things are of good report;
if there be any virtue, if there be any praise,
think on these things.

PHILIPPIANS 4:8 (1ST CENTURY)

When the vision of Reality comes, the veil of ignorance is completely removed. As long as we perceive things falsely, our false perception distracts us and makes us miserable. When our false perception is corrected, misery ends also.

SHANKARA (9TH CENTURY)

Two men look out through the same bars: one sees the mud, and one the stars.

FREDERICK LANGBRIDGE (19TH CENTURY)

People are always blaming their
circumstances for what they are. I don't
believe in circumstances. The people who
get on in this world are the people who get
up and look for the circumstances they want;
and if they can't find them, make them.

GEORGE BERNARD SHAW (19TH–20TH CENTURY)

Man is what he believes.

ANTON CHEKHOV (19TH CENTURY)

Life consists in what a man is thinking of
all day.

RALPH WALDO EMERSON (19TH CENTURY)

Peace is not an absence of war, it is a virtue,
a state of mind, a disposition for
benevolence, confidence, justice.

BARUCH SPINOZA (17TH CENTURY)

It is the mind which maketh good or ill
That maketh wretch or happy, rich or poor.

EDMUND SPENSER (16TH CENTURY)

I do not mean to gloss over or discount
the very real suffering in this world.
Nevertheless, when something bad happens
and we feel we have no control over the
tragedy itself, we still have some control
over our responses. We can lash out in
bitterness and anger against the unfairness
of life that has deprived us of pleasure and
joy. Or, we can look for good in unexpected
sources, even our apparent enemies.

PHILIP YANCEY (20TH CENTURY)

Five

❦

LET IT GO –
PUT THE PAST BEHIND YOU

IF WE ARE TO LIVE IN THE PRESENT MOMENT WE HAVE to live with an open mind, not one that is full of preconceptions and attachments, and certainly not one that clings to the past. Letting go is one of life's hardest tasks. We become attached to so much – to those we love, to our possessions, to our jobs and status, to our opinions, our looks, our memories ... Our attachments ultimately lead to suffering, for we are destined one way or another to lose those things or people we are attached to.

We also find it difficult to let go of hurts, injustice, betrayal and tragedy in our lives. We tend to carry the wounds and scars, along with damaging behaviour patterns, rather than letting them go. Anger, resentment, guilt get in the way of living in the present, preventing us from getting on with our lives and growing as human beings.

What lies at the root of this unnecessary burden is a failure to forgive. When we are unable to forgive and let go of the pain, we become prisoners to the past and are unavailable to the present, and the future. We turn in on ourselves and our lives and relationships can become blocked or unfulfilled. If we're to make a new beginning, we have to wipe the slate clean; die to the past and be reborn – easier said than done, of course. We all know how impossibly difficult it can be to forgive – either ourselves for something we have done wrong, or another for the hurt they have caused us, or life itself for the hand it has dealt us. But punishing ourselves or another by our unwillingness or inability to forgive is damaging to all concerned. Depression, low self-esteem, illness and addictions are a high price to pay for hanging on to the past.

All the great religious traditions have dealt with forgiveness, and each tradition has its own method for dealing with it – prayer, repentance, chanting, good works or belief in future lives to dispel the karma of past actions. All religions agree that guilt is a heavy burden. So clearly we should do all we can, as we face the future, to lighten our load. If we can rise above the pain and guilt of the past, everything begins to look different. We become more open to life and the present moment. When we heal the wounds of the past, peace of mind is our reward.

Letting go means just what it says. It's an invitation to cease clinging to anything – whether it be an idea, a thing, an event, a particular time, or view or desire. It is a conscious decision to release with full acceptance into the stream of present moments as they are unfolding. To let go means to give up coercing, resisting or struggling, in exchange for something more powerful and wholesome which comes out of allowing things to be as they are without getting caught up in your attraction to or rejection of them, in the intrinsic stickiness of wanting, of liking and disliking. It's akin to letting your palm open to unhand something you have been holding on to.

JOHN KABAT-ZINN (20TH CENTURY)

Without freedom from the past there is no
freedom at all, because the mind is never
new, fresh, innocent. It is only the fresh,
innocent mind that is free.

KRISHNAMURTI (20TH CENTURY)

Our mind should be free from the traces of
the past, just like the flowers of spring.

SHUNRYU SUZUKI-ROSHI (20TH CENTURY)

There is only one courage and that is the
courage to go on dying to the past, not to
collect it, not to accumulate it, not to cling
to it. We all cling to the past, and because
we cling to the past we become unavailable
to the present.

OSHO (20TH CENTURY)

It is only by acknowledging impermanence that there is the chance to die and the space to be reborn and the possibility of appreciating life as a creative process.

CHOGYAM TRUNGPA (20TH CENTURY)

To be a traveller on this earth, you must know how to die and come to life again.

JOHANN WOLFGANG GOETHE (18TH–19TH CENTURY)

A man must die; that is, he must free himself from a thousand petty attachments and identifications ... He is attached to everything in his life, attached to his imagination, attached to his stupidity, attached even to his sufferings, possibly to his sufferings more than to anything else. ... Attachments to things, identification with things, keep alive a thousand useless 'I's in a man. These 'I's must die in order that the big I may be born. But how can they be made to die? They do not want to die. It is at this point that the possibility of awakening comes to the rescue. To awaken means to realize one's nothingness.

G. I. GURDJIEFF (20TH CENTURY)

What is born will die,

What has been gathered will be dispersed,

What has accumulated will be exhausted,

What has been built up will collapse,

And what has been high will be brought low.

THE BUDDHA (6TH CENTURY BC)

He who binds to himself a Joy,

Does the winged life destroy;

He, who kisses the Joy as it flies,

Lives in Eternity's sunrise.

WILLIAM BLAKE (18TH–19TH CENTURY)

Except a man be born again,

he cannot see the kingdom of God.

JOHN 3:3 (1ST CENTURY)

As long as we are confined by our previous experience, we limit our possibilities for change. Recognizing that the power of transformation lies in the present moment allows the space for creative movement. If we remain focused in the present, neither lost in the past nor projecting into the future, then it becomes possible to muster our full energies toward creativity. Such an engagement with life moves us out of identification with our small self and into co-creation with the universe.

JUSTINE WILLIS TOMS AND MICHAEL TOMS
(20TH CENTURY)

Be not the slave of your own past – plunge
into the sublime seas, dive deep, and swim
far, so you shall come back with self-respect,
with new power, with an advanced
experience, that shall explain and overlook
the old.

RALPH WALDO EMERSON (19TH CENTURY)

It is the process of accumulation that creates habit, imitation, and for the mind that accumulates there is deterioration, death. But a mind that is not accumulating, not gathering, that is dying every day, every minute – for such a mind there is no death. It is in a state of infinite space.

So the mind must die to everything it has gathered – to all the habits, the imitated virtues, to all the things that it has relied on for its sense of security. Then it is no longer caught in the net of its own thinking. In dying to the past from moment to moment the mind is made fresh, therefore it can never deteriorate or set in motion the wave of darkness.

J. KRISHNAMURTI (20TH CENTURY)

We are what we believe. Our belief system is based on our past experience which is constantly being relived in the present, with an anticipation of the future being like the past. Our present perceptions are so coloured by the past that we are unable to see the immediate happenings in our lives without distortions and limitations. With willingness, we can re-examine who we think we are in order to achieve a new and deeper sense of real identity.

GERALD G. JAMPOLSKY (20TH CENTURY)

One discovers that destiny can be directed,
that one does not have to remain in bondage
to the first wax imprint made in childhood.
Once the deforming mirror is smashed,
there is a possibility of wholeness; there
is a possibility of joy.

ANAÏS NIN (20TH CENTURY)

We know what we feel,

know what we desire,

then slowly surrender

to accept what is, and forgive.

What might have been

the salt of bitterness

becomes the salt of wisdom.

MARION WOODMAN (20TH CENTURY)

The unforgiving mind is full of fear,

and offers love no room to be itself;

no place where it can spread its wings in peace

and soar above the turmoil of the world.

The unforgiving mind is sad,

without the hope of respite and release from pain.

It suffers and abides in misery,

peering about in darkness, seeing not,

yet certain of the danger lurking there.

A COURSE IN MIRACLES (20TH CENTURY)

Sinners are mirrors: when we see faults in
them, we must realize that they only reflect
the evil in us.

BA'AL SHEM TOV (ISAEL BEN ELEAZAR) (18TH CENTURY)

It is easy to see the faults of others,
but difficult to see one's own faults.
One shows the faults of others like chaff
    winnowed in the wind,
but one conceals one's own faults as a cunning
    gambler conceals his dice.

THE DHAMMAPADA (6TH CENTURY BC)

If we could read the secret history of our
enemies, we should find in each man's life
sorrow and suffering enough to disarm all
hostility.

HENRY WADSWORTH LONGFELLOW (19TH CENTURY)

Never preen yourself
that you are prideless;
for pride is more invisible
than an ant's footprint
on a black stone
in the dark of night.

JAMI (15TH CENTURY)

We must be willing to get rid of the life
we've planned, so as to have the life that is
waiting for us. The old skin has to be shed
before the new one can come.

JOSEPH CAMPBELL (20TH CENTURY)

God forgives all sins.

THE KORAN (7TH CENTURY)

❧

One should forgive under any injury.

THE MAHABHARATA (4TH–5TH CENTURY BC)

❧

Forgiveness is the answer to the child's dream
of a miracle by which what is broken is made
whole again, what is soiled is made clean.

DAG HAMMARSKJÖLD (20TH CENTURY)

❧

Let none find fault in others. Let none see
omissions and commissions in others. But
let one see one's own act, done and undone.

THE DHAMMAPADA (6TH CENTURY BC)

73

Do not weep; do not wax indignant.
Understand.

BARUCH SPINOZA (17TH CENTURY)

To live without forgiveness is to live separated
from the sacred and from the most basic
instincts of our heart. To live with forgiveness
is to choose in each moment an active role in
creating relationships, organizations, communities and a world that works for everyone.

ROBIN CASARJIAN (20TH CENTURY)

Inner peace can be reached only when we practice forgiveness. Forgiveness is the letting go of the past, and is therefore the means for correcting our misperceptions.

Our misperceptions can only be undone *now*, and can be accomplished only through letting go whatever we think other people have done to us, or whatever we think we have done to them. Through this process of selective forgetting, we become free to embrace a present without the need to re-enact our past.

GERALD G. JAMPOLSKY (20TH CENTURY)

Six

TRUST THE UNIVERSE — FAITH IS THE ANSWER

AS WE LOOK TOWARDS THE FUTURE, THERE IS SO LITTLE that we can feel any certainty about. Change is constant, nothing remains the same for long. And as the pace of change seems to grow ever faster, it's easy to feel over-whelmed. Because of the secular nature of our society, and the domination of our culture by a sound-bite media which has little time for genuine spirituality, faith is regarded as something deeply unfashionable.

But, life is a great mystery, and if we put our trust in materialism, we are ultimately going to feel empty, let down and betrayed by an unpredictable world. We need to live by faith, to feel that there exists a power greater than ourselves – nature, the Universe, Spirit, God – whatever term we use, and to accept that we cannot know all the answers. When we allow ourselves to feel that reverence for a creative power at the heart of the universe, and to trust the unfolding of life's process, and that this power is always there and will support us, faith grows.

All the major religious traditions emphasize the importance of faith. It is like an anchor in a restless sea. The mind wants to know what lies ahead, how we will cope, but the discipline (for indeed it is a discipline) of faith teaches us to be patient and to trust. In the words of the fourteenth-century English mystic, Julian of Norwich – 'all shall be well, all shall be well, and all manner of things shall be well.' Time and again we find if we can hold on, trusting the Universe, then assistance comes, we are not totally abandoned, however hopeless the situation might appear. Miracles happen.

We have to work hard at faith – difficult in times of hardship or unhappiness, but when we do, we reap its rewards. Without it, life is almost impossibly hard to bear at times, and it is essential if our hopes and dreams are to stand a chance of being realized.

Faith is to believe what you do not yet see;
the reward for this faith is to see what you
believe.

SAINT AUGUSTINE (4TH–5TH CENTURY)

I never saw a moor,
I never saw the sea;
Yet I know how the heather looks,
And what a wave must be.
I never spoke with God
Nor visited him in heaven;
Yet certain am I of the spot
As if the chart were given.

EMILY DICKINSON (19TH CENTURY)

God is not far from the seeker,

nor is it impossible to see Him.

He is like the sun, which is ever shining right

    above you.

        MEHER BABA (20TH CENTURY)

                  ❧

It is cynicism and fear that freeze life; it is

faith that thaws it out, releases it, sets it free.

   HARRY EMERSON FOSDICK (20TH CENTURY)

                  ❧

Believe to the end, even if all men went

    astray and you were left the only one

faithful; bring your offering even then and

    praise God in your loneliness.

    FYODOR DOSTOEVSKY (19TH CENTURY)

Let nothing disturb thee, nothing afright thee;
All things are passing, God never changes.
Patient endurance attaineth to all things.
Who God possesses in nothing is wanting;
Alone God suffices.

SAINT TERESA OF AVILA (16TH CENTURY)

God, take me by Your Hand. I shall follow
you dutifully, and not resist too much. I shall
evade none of the tempest life has in store
for me. I shall try to face it all as best I can ...
I shall never again assume, in my innocence,
that any peace that comes my way will be
eternal. I shall accept all the inevitable
tumult and struggle ... I shall follow
wherever Your hand leads me and shall
try not to be afraid.

ETTY HILLESUM (20TH CENTURY)

All that I have seen teaches me to trust the
Creator for all I have not seen.

RALPH WALDO EMERSON (19TH CENTURY)

I see the world gradually being turned into a
    wilderness.
I can feel the suffering of millions and yet,
if I look up to the heavens, I think it will all come
    right,
that this cruelty too will end, and that peace and
tranquility will return again.

ANNE FRANK (20TH CENTURY)

If you have faith as a grain of mustard-seed,
    you shall say to this mountain, 'Move hence
        to yonder place;' and it shall move; and
            nothing shall be impossible unto you.

MATTHEW 17:20 (1ST CENTURY)

That faith is of little value which can flourish
only in fair weather. Faith in order to be of
any value must survive the severest of trials.

M. K. GANDHI (20TH CENTURY)

He who perceives Me everywhere, and
beholds everything in Me never loses sight
of Me nor do I ever lose sight of him.

THE BHAGAVAD GITA
(2ND CENTURY BC – 2ND CENTURY AD)

Lo! I am with you always, even unto the
end of the world.

MATTHEW 28:20 (1ST CENTURY)

The winds of grace are blowing all the time.
You have only to raise your sail.

RAMAKRISHNA (19TH CENTURY)

Faith furnishes prayer with wings, without
which it cannot soar to Heaven.

SAINT JOHN CLIMACUS (6TH CENTURY)

Nothing in this world is so marvellous as the
transformation that a soul undergoes when
the light of faith descends upon the light of
reason.

W. BERNARD ULLATHORNE (19TH CENTURY)

Here you speak to me

Most clearly

Amidst this

Sea of green

Bedded with pinks and purple

So beautiful this year

After several seasons

of slow growth.

Here in the garden

of my planting

And your watering

You assure me that

All will be well.

KATHY KEAY (20TH CENTURY)

God is our refuge and strength, a very present help
    in trouble.
Therefore will we not fear, though the earth be
    removed, and the mountains be carried to the
    midst of the sea.

PSALM 46:1–2 (8TH–3RD CENTURY BC)

Allah is with those who patiently endure.

THE KORAN (7TH CENTURY)

But doubt is as crucial to faith as darkness is
to light. Without one, the other has no con-
text and is meaningless. Faith is, by defini-
tion, uncertainty. It is full of doubt, steeped
in risk. It is about matters not of the known
but of the unknown.

CARTER HEYWOOD (20TH CENTURY)

... faith gives us the courage to go from the familiarity of the known to the unknown. Faith enables us to forsake the sanctuaries of our security and boundaries and to reach for new and unfamiliar horizons. We need faith, too, to reach toward and understand that which is greater than ourselves: faith in the universal law that governs the seasons and creates the forms of life and brings us to consciousness; faith that there is an underlying oneness in the multiplicity we perceive; faith that there is a universal truth and freedom that is the territory of no one person.

When all else seems to fall away or is taken away from us, we fall back upon this faith to take us through the dark, confused, or difficult places in our life. Faith brings us the energy, trust, and inspiration to face those places and to awaken to their truths rather than running from them. This faith can be inspired by great books, by great teachers of the past, or by great deeds, but in the end this faith is found primarily in ourselves. Here is where our wisdom grows, where the truth reveals itself.

JACK KORNFIELD AND CHRISTINA FELDMAN
(20TH CENTURY)

~

The state of faith allows no mention of impossibility.

TERTULLIAN (2ND CENTURY)

~

You know that if you get in the water and have nothing to hold on to, but try to behave as you would on dry land, you will drown. But if, on the other hand, you trust yourself to the water and let go you will float. And this is exactly the situation of faith.

ALAN WATTS (20TH CENTURY)

The Faith of every man accords with his
essential nature; man here is made up of
faith; as a man's faith is, so is he.

BHAGAVAD GITA (2ND CENTURY BC – 2ND CENTURY AD)

Faith is the antiseptic of the soul.

WALT WHITMAN (19TH CENTURY)

Seven

~≫~

LISTEN, AND PAY ATTENTION — YOU WILL HEAR THE STILL SMALL VOICE

IF WE WANT TO BREAK THE HOLD WHICH TIME HAS ON US, there is nothing better we can do than sit still and be silent. If we want to live differently, and if we want a more peaceful world, we have to stop, be silent and pay attention.

When we sit and listen, inspiration comes to us. Artists, writers and composers, have often testified to the necessity of silence and solitude for their creative endeavours. The mystics have always understood the value of silence – The Desert Fathers went out into the wilderness, the holymen of India went into the forests and the monks and nuns into the cloisters.

But just as much for you and me, at the end of the twentieth century, sitting still and listening can pay enormous dividends. When we sit quietly, we allow our intuition to bubble up, and that intuition is no less than the life-force itself. We need to practise listening and attuning ourselves to this inner voice of guidance, trusting what we hear. And although we are not necessarily thinking about our problems, as if by magic, an answer to them comes.

When we habitually set aside time to be quiet and simply listen, a new awareness develops. As we experience the peace that comes from within, 'the peace that passeth all understanding', we get a fresh perspective on our lives and are more able to come to terms with whatever is going on in them. And the more we experience peace, which is after all what we really long for deep down, the more we ourselves manifest peace in our lives.

Do you have the patience to wait till your mud settles and the water is clear? Can you remain unmoving till the right action arises by itself?

LAO TZU (4TH CENTURY)

A desire arises in the mind. It is satisfied; immediately another comes. In the interval which separates two desires a perfect calm reigns in the mind. It is at this moment freed from all thought, love or hate. Complete peace equally reigns between two mental waves.

SWAMI SIVANANDA (20TH CENTURY)

All men's miseries derive from not being
able to sit quiet in a room alone.

BLAISE PASCAL

Quiet minds cannot be perplexed or fright-
ened, but go on in fortune or misfortune at
their own private pace, like a clock during
a thunderstorm.

ROBERT LOUIS STEVENSON (19TH CENTURY)

Silence is the perfectest herald of joy.

WILLIAM SHAKESPEARE (16TH CENTURY)

You do not need to leave your room ...
Remain sitting at your table and listen. Do
not even listen, simply wait. Do not even
wait, be quite still and solitary. The world
will freely offer itself to you to be
unmasked. It has no choice. It will roll in
ecstasy at your feet.

FRANZ KAFKA (20TH CENTURY)

Those who seek the truth by means of intel-
lect and learning only get further and
further away from it. Not till your thoughts
cease all their branching here and there, not
till you abandon all thoughts of seeking for
something, not till your mind is motionless
as wood or stone, will you be on the right
road to the Gate.

HUANG PO (9TH CENTURY)

... only when we are silent can we begin to hear the voice that is truly our own – what the Quakers call 'the still small voice within' ... The source of this voice – which may be without sound, and yet is heard – is called by many different names: the inner guide, guardian angel, spirit guide, the collective unconscious, or just plain intuition. Actually all of us hear the whisperings of this voice every single day of our lives, but many ignore it.

RICK FIELDS (20TH CENTURY)

To a mind that is still
The whole universe surrenders.

CHUANG TZU (3RD CENTURY)

Learn to be silent. Let your quiet mind
listen and absorb.

PYTHAGORAS (6TH CENTURY BC)

Listen in deep silence.
Be very still and open your mind ...
Sink deep into the peace that waits for you
beyond the frantic, riotous thoughts
and sights and sounds of this insane world.

A COURSE IN MIRACLES (20TH CENTURY)

We do not need any deep metaphysics: we
need to understand the simple little truth
that the still small voice is the power that
destroys the illusions of this world.

JOEL S. GOLDSMITH (20TH CENTURY)

We spend most of our time and energy in a kind of horizontal thinking. We move along the surface of things going from one quick base to another, often with a frenzy that wears us out. We collect data, things, people, ideas, 'profound experiences', never penetrating any of them ... But there are other times. There are times when we stop. We sit still. We lose ourselves in a pile of leaves or its memory. We listen and breezes from a whole other world begin to whisper.

JAMES CARROLL (20TH CENTURY)

The moment one gives close attention to anything, even a blade of grass, it becomes a mysterious, awesome, indescribably magnificent world in itself.

HENRY MILLER (20TH CENTURY)

Truth is within ourselves; it takes no rise

From outward things whate'er you may believe.

There is an inmost centre in us all,

Where truth abides in fullness; and around,

Wall upon wall, the gross flesh hems it in,

This perfect, clear perception – which is truth.

A baffling and perverting carnal mesh

Binds it, and makes all error; and to know

Rather consists in opening out a way

Whence the imprisoned splendour may escape,

Than in effecting entry for a light

Supposed to be without.

ROBERT BROWNING (19TH CENTURY)

He who goes to the bottom of his own heart

knows his own nature;

and knowing his own nature, he knows heaven.

MENCIUS (3RD CENTURY BC)

He who knows others is discerning,

but he who knows himself is enlightened.

LAO TZU (4TH CENTURY BC)

❧

Be still and know that I am God.

PSALM 46:10

❧

Let us become silent

that we may hear the whispers of the gods ...

There is guidance for each of us,

and by lowly listening we shall hear the right word.

RALPH WALDO EMERSON (19TH CENTURY)

❧

Go to your bosom;

knock there, and ask your heart what it doth know.

WILLIAM SHAKESPEARE
MEASURE FOR MEASURE PART II: ACT II
(16TH CENTURY)

Stop talking, stop thinking,

and there is nothing you will not understand.

Return to the root and you will find the meaning;

Pursue the light and you lose its source.

Look inward and in a flash you will conquer

the apparent and the void.

All come from mistaken views.

There is no need to seek the truth, only stop

    having views.

      SENG TS'AN (SOSAN) (6TH CENTURY)

Keep thyself first in peace,

and then thou wilt be able to bring others to peace.

      THOMAS Á KEMPIS (15TH CENTURY)

    Certain thoughts are prayers. There are

    moments when, whatever be the attitude of

    the body, the soul is on its knees.

      VICTOR HUGO (19TH CENTURY)

More things are wrought by prayer
Than this world dreams of.

ALFRED, LORD TENNYSON (19TH CENTURY)

❧

You pray in your distress and in your need:
would that you might pray also in the
fullness of your joy and in your days of
abundance.

KAHLIL GIBRAN (20TH CENTURY)

❧

When man closes his lips, it is then that God
speaks.

HAZRAT INAYAT KHAN (20TH CENTURY)

❧

Peace comes within the souls of men
When they realize their oneness with the universe.

BLACK ELK (20TH CENTURY)

We have to learn to listen in different ways
and in different places: in silence and in
noise. Perhaps it is because so many people
have lost the art of listening that they have
also lost the ability to pray.

SHEILA CASSIDY (20TH CENTURY)

Praying is not about asking; it's about
listening.

CHAGDUD TULKU RINPOCHE (20TH CENTURY)

Paradise is nearer to you than the thongs of
your sandals.

THE KORAN (7TH CENTURY)

I gazed into my heart

There I saw Him; He was nowhere else.

JALAL AL-DIN RUMI (13TH CENTURY)

Are you looking for me? I am in the next seat.

My shoulder is against yours.

You will not find me in stupas, nor in Indian shrine

rooms, nor in synagogues, nor in cathedrals;

not in masses nor kirtans,

not in legs winding around your neck,

nor in eating nothing but vegetables.

When you really look for me, you will see me

instantly –

you will find me in the tiniest house of time.

Kabir says: Student, tell me, what is God?

He is the breath inside the breath.

KABIR (15TH CENTURY)

When each day

is sacred

when each hour

is sacred

when each instant

is sacred

earth and you

space and you

bearing the sacred

through time

you'll reach

the fields of light.

GUILLEVIC (20TH CENTURY)

As my prayer became more attentive and inward I had less and less to say. I finally became completely silent. I started to listen – which is even further removed from speaking. I first thought that praying entailed speaking. I then learnt that praying is hearing, not merely being silent. This is how it is. To pray does not mean to listen to oneself speaking. Prayer involves becoming silent, and being silent, and waiting until God is heard.

SOREN KIERKEGAARD (19TH CENTURY)

Eight

❧

COUNT YOUR BLESSINGS — AND BE SURPRISED BY JOY

LIFE IS A GIFT, BUT ALL TOO OFTEN WE TAKE IT FOR granted, never realizing until something unpleasant or tragic happens, just how fragile it all is. For the most part, unless we are extremely fortunate, life is difficult, and we try to steer a course between the rocks and whirlpools as we head towards our own particular paradise. As we cope with what life throws at us, good and bad, gratitude for what we have is a wonderful discipline to practise. To wake in the morning, grateful for a night's rest and the new day that's dawned, regardless of our circumstances, is far from easy. When we are sick, or troubled, or worse – it's hard even to notice, let alone appreciate, all the wonder of life that surrounds us – sun, rain, sky, the view before us, a touch, a smile, food, water, or an exquisite piece of music ... But in taking time to remember what we do have in our lives, it's as if we have switched on a light in the darkness. By adopting an attitude of appreciation we open up our hearts and become a conduit for good things to come into our lives. Counting our blessings is an attitude which enables us to understand that we are fortunate to be here, participating in this extraordinary unfolding universe, and the result is joy.

Joy, which is not the same as pleasure, is a gift, sparked by the recognition of something which moves us, makes us feel connected to something greater than ourselves, and that all's well with the world, in spite of its horrors and tragedies.

But what about the obverse side of the coin – sorrow? Strange as it many seem, there too lies a gift of sorts. Most of us would rather avoid pain and suffering, but when adversity strikes, as indeed it does all too frequently, we find that in confronting it and dealing with it we are changed. Through pain (whether it is physical or emotional) we can learn to cope, and even to triumph. Pain and sorrow open us up so that our capacity for joy is greater than ever.

Reflect upon your present blessings, of
which every man has many; not on your past
misfortunes, of which all men have some.

CHARLES DICKENS (19TH CENTURY)

Look to this day

For it is life, the very life of life

In its brief course

Lie all the verities and realities of your existence:

The bliss of growth

The glory of action

The splendour of beauty

For yesterday is but a dream

And tomorrow is only a vision,

But today well lived

makes every yesterday a dream of happiness

And every tomorrow a vision of hope.

Look well, therefore to this day!

Such is the salutation to the dawn.

KALIDASA (4TH CENTURY BC – 2ND CENTURY AD)

We do not understand that life is paradise,
for it suffices only to wish to understand it,
and at once paradise will appear in front of
us in its beauty.

FYODOR DOSTOEVSKY (19TH CENTURY)

The soul should always stand ajar, ready to
welcome the ecstatic experience.

EMILY DICKINSON (19TH CENTURY)

Glance at the sun.

See the moon and the stars.

Gaze at the beauty of earth's greenings

Now,

think.

What delight

God gives

to humankind

with all these things

Who gives all these shining,

wonderful gifts, if not God?

HILDEGARD OF BINGEN (12TH CENTURY)

When you arise in the morning, give thanks
for the morning light, for your life and
strength. Give thanks for your food and the
joy of living. If you see no reason for giving
thanks, the fault lies in yourself.

TECUMSEH (19TH CENTURY)

The great sea has set me in motion.
Set me adrift,
And I move as a weed in the river.

The arch of sky
And mightiness of storms
Encompasses me,
And I am left
Trembling with joy.

ESKIMO SONG

Dance, my heart! Dance today with joy.
The strains of love fill the days and the nights with
   music, and the world is listening to its
   melodies:
Mad with joy, life and death dance to the rhythms
   of this music. The hills and the sea and the
   earth dance.
The world of men dances in laughter and tears.
Why put on the robe of the monk, and live aloof
   from the world in lonely pride?
Behold! My heart dances in delight of a hundred
   arts: and the Creator is well pleased.

KABIR (15TH CENTURY)

You are surrounded by gifts every living
moment of every day. Let yourself feel
appreciation for their presence in your life
and take the time to acknowledge their
splendour.

LOU G. NUNGESSER (20TH CENTURY)

If life gave us at one time everything we wanted, such as wealth, power and friends, we would sooner or later become tired of them; but there is one thing that can never become stale to us: joy itself.

PARAMAHANSA YOGANANDA (19TH CENTURY)

In bliss these creatures are born, in bliss they are sustained, and to bliss they merge again.

THE VEDAS (1500–2000 BC)

Gratitude goes hand in hand with love, and where one is the other must be found.

A COURSE IN MIRACLES (20TH CENTURY)

Think of your life as if it were a banquet where you would behave graciously. When dishes are passed to you, extend your hand and help yourself to a moderate portion. If a dish should pass you by, enjoy what is already on your plate. Or if the dish hasn't been passed to you yet, patiently wait your turn.

Carry over this same attitude of polite restraint and gratitude to your children, spouse, career, and finances. There is no need to yearn, envy, and grab. You will get your rightful portion when it is your time.

EPICTETUS (1ST–2ND CENTURY)

If there is a sin against life, it consists perhaps not so much in despairing of life as in hoping for another life and in eluding the implacable grandeur of this life.

ALBERT CAMUS (20TH CENTURY)

Take away all from me, but leave me Ecstasy,
And I am richer than all my fellow men.

EMILY DICKINSON (19TH CENTURY)

God respects me when I work,
but He loves me when I sing.

RABINDRANATH TAGORE (19TH–20TH CENTURY)

Whatever joy there is in this world
All comes from desiring others to be happy
And whatever suffering there is in this world
All comes from desiring myself to be happy.

SHANTIDEVA (8TH CENTURY)

I was utterly alone with the sun and the earth. Lying down on the grass, I spoke in my soul to the earth, the sun, and the air, and the distant sea far beyond sight. ... With all the intensity of feelings which exalted me, all the intense communion ... in no manner can the thrilling depth of these feelings be written – with these I prayed, as if they were the keys of an instrument, of an organ, with which I swelled forth the notes of my soul, redoubling my own voice by their power.

RICHARD JEFFERIES (19TH CENTURY)

Rejoice always, pray without ceasing, in everything give thanks.

1 THESSALONIANS 5:16–18 (1ST CENTURY)

i thank you God for most this amazing day: for the
    leaping greenly spirits of trees and a blue true
    dream of sky; and for everything which is nat-
    ural which is infinite which is yes.
(i who have died am alive again today, and this is
    the sun's birthday; this is the birth day of life
    and of love and wings and of the gay great
    happening illimitably earth)
how should tasting touching hearing seeing
    breathing any – lifted from the no of all noth-
    ing – human merely being doubt
    unimaginable You?
(now the ears of my ears awake and now the eyes
    of my eyes are opened)

E E CUMMINGS (20TH CENTURY)

Gratitude is heaven itself.

WILLIAM BLAKE (18TH–19TH CENTURY)

Weeping may endure for a night, but joy cometh
in the morning.

PSALM 30:5

Every day is a god, each day is a god,
and holiness holds forth in time.
I worship each god,
I praise each day splintered down,
and wrapped in time like a husk,
a hush of many colours spreading,
at dawn fast over the mountain split.

ANNIE DILLARD (20TH CENTURY)

O come, let us sing unto the Lord: let us make a
joyful noise to the rock of our salvation.

Let us come before his presence with
thanksgiving, and make a joyful noise unto
him with psalms.

For the Lord is a great God, and a great King
above all gods.

In his hands are the deep places of the earth: the
strength of the hills is his also.

The sea is his, and he made it: and his hands
formed the dry land.

O come, let us worship and bow down: let us kneel
before the Lord our maker.

PSALM 95:1–6

I'm filled with joy

when the day dawns quietly

over the roof of the sky.

Life was wonderful

in winter.

But did winter make me happy?

No, I always worried

about hides for boot-soles

and for boots,

and if there'd be enough

for all of us.

Yes, I worried constantly.

Life was wonderful

in summer.

But did summer make me happy?

No, I always worried

about reindeer skins and rugs for the platform.

Yes, I worried constantly.

Life was wonderful

when you stood at your fishing-hole

on the ice

But was I happy waiting at my fishing hole?

No, I was always worried

for my little hook,

in case it never got a bite.

Yes, I worried constantly.

Life was wonderful

when you danced in the feasting-house.

But did this make me any happier?

No, I always worried

I'd forget my song.

Yes, I worried constantly.

Life was wonderful ...

And I still feel joy

each time the day-break

whitens the dark sky

each time the sun

climbs over the roof of the sky.

ESKIMO SONG (20TH CENTURY)

A thankful heart is not only the greatest virtue,
But the parent of all other virtues.

MARCUS TULLIUS CICERO (1ST CENTURY BC)

So I will go about Your altar, O Lord,
That I may pray with the voice of thanksgiving,
And tell of Your wondrous works.

PSALM 26:7 (8TH–3RD CENTURY BC)

God has two dwellings, one in heaven and
the other in a meek and thankful heart.

IZAAK WALTON (17TH CENTURY)

I will give thanks unto thee, for I am
fearfully and wonderfully made.

1662 PRAYER BOOK

Your light, my light, world-filling light, the dancing
   centre of my life, the sky breaks forth, the
   wind runs wild, and laughter passes over the
   earth.
The butterflies have spread their sails to glide up
   on the seas of light; the lilies and the jasmine
   flowers surge on the crest of waves of light.
Now heaven's river drowns its banks, and floods of
   joy have run abroad; now mirth has spread
   from leaf to leaf, and gladness without
   measure comes.

RABINDRANATH TAGORE (19TH–20TH CENTURY)

We return thanks to our mother, the earth,

which sustains us.

We return thanks to the rivers and streams,

which supply us with water.

We return thanks to all herbs,

which furnish medicines for the cure of our diseases.

We return thanks to the corn, and to her sisters,

the beans and squashes,

which give us life.

We return thanks to the wind,

which, moving the air

has banished diseases.

We return thanks to the moon and stars,

which have given to us their light when the sun was
    gone.

We return thanks to the sun,

that he has looked upon the earth with a beneficent
    eye.

Lastly, we return thanks to the Great Spirit,

in whom is embodied all goodness,

and who directs all things for the good of his children.

IROQUOIS PRAYER (20TH CENTURY)

To bless means to wish, unconditionally, total, unrestricted good for others and events from the deepest chamber of your heart: it means to hallow, to hold in reverence, to behold with utter awe that which is always a gift from the Creator. He who is hallowed by your blessing is set aside, consecrated, holy, whole. To bless is yet to invoke divine care upon, to speak or think gratefully for, to confer happiness upon – although we ourselves are never the bestower, but simply the joyful witnesses of life's abundance.

To bless all without discrimination of any sort is the ultimate form of giving, because those you bless will never know from whence came the sudden ray that burst through the clouds of their skies, and you will rarely be a witness to the sunlight in their lives.

PIERRE PRADERVAND (20TH CENTURY)

Everywhere a greater joy is preceded by a greater suffering.

Saint Augustine (4th–5th century)

It was only when I lay there on rotting prison straw that I sensed within myself the first stirrings of good. Gradually, it was disclosed to me that the line separating good and evil passes not through states, nor between classes, not between political parties either – but right through every human heart – and through all human hearts ... I nourished my soul there, and I say without hesitation: Bless you, prison, for having been in my life.

Alexander Solzhenitsyn (20th century)

Nine

❧

TRY A LITTLE KINDNESS —
COMPASSION IS THE KEY

AS WE MOVE FORWARD INTO A NEW ERA, ONE QUALITY amongst those we need to develop is paramount – compassion. It's something which all the great humanitarians and teachers of different religious traditions have stressed since the dawn of history. Compassion is the key, a kind of cosmic glue that holds the universe together. We are not separate – whatever the ego may think! – but part of the whole, as science is now beginning to demonstrate. And if we are, then how we behave and think, and what we do, has an effect on the whole. We can make a difference. So practising compassion makes a lot of sense.

But how can we feel love and empathy, and behave accordingly, when all about us may seem dark and hopeless? Simply by making a conscious decision to be more loving, and by constant practice. And that may not be as arduous as it sounds – for we begin with ourselves, taking time for ourselves, caring for ourselves, nurturing our minds and bodies with what is life-enhancing. This is not narcissistic or selfish. The truth is that if we feel good ourselves and truly accept who we are, then we are more able to be compassionate to others. We can more readily love our neighbour as ourselves. By being gentle with ourselves, we are much more able to empathize with another's pain. A kind word, a helping hand, the offering of oneself, in terms of time and effort, are the natural outcome of loving oneself, they are not the result of rushing around 'doing good'.

And as we give love away, it comes back to us and makes our lives joyous and meaningful. Compassion, for oneself and others, requires practice, and as we practise we become wiser and more fulfilled.

Waking up this morning, I smile. Twenty-four brand new hours are before me. I vow to live fully in each moment and to look at all beings with eyes of compassion.

THICH NHAT HANH (20TH CENTURY)

Wherever there is a human being, there is an opportunity for kindness.

SENECA (1ST CENTURY)

Three things in human life are important. The first is to be kind, the second is to be kind and the third is to be kind!

HENRY JAMES (19TH CENTURY)

My religion is very simple. My religion is
kindness.

TENZIN GYATSO, THE FOURTEENTH
DALAI LAMA OF TIBET (20TH CENTURY)

One must learn to care for oneself first,
so that one can then dare care for someone
else. That's what it takes to make the caged
bird sing.

MAYA ANGELOU (20TH CENTURY)

A man cannot be comfortable without his
own approval.

MARK TWAIN (19TH CENTURY)

Compassion is a natural feeling, which, by moderating the violence of love of self in each individual, contributes to the preservation of the whole species. It is this compassion that hurries us without reflection to the relief of those who are in distress.

JEAN-JACQUES ROUSSEAU (18TH CENTURY)

You must love yourself before you love another. By accepting yourself and fully being what you are ... your simple presence can make others happy.

JANE ROBERTS (20TH CENTURY)

I celebrate myself, and sing myself ...
I am larger, better than I thought.
I did not know I held so much goodness.

WALT WHITMAN (19TH CENTURY)

A human being is part of the whole called by us a universe – a part limited in time and space. He experiences himself, his thoughts and his feelings, as something separate from the rest, a kind of optical delusion of his consciousness.

This delusion is a kind of prison for us; it restricts us to our personal decisions and our affections to a few persons nearest to us.

Our task must be to free ourselves from this prison by widening our circle of compassion to embrace all living creatures and the whole of nature in its beauty.

ALBERT EINSTEIN (19TH–20TH CENTURY)

The unity that binds us together, that makes this earth a family and all men brothers and sons of God, is love.

THOMAS WOLFE (19TH–20TH CENTURY)

If there is any kindness I can show, or any good thing I can do to any fellow being, let me do it now, and not deter or neglect it, as I shall not pass this way again.

WILLIAM PENN (17TH CENTURY)

Now, although I have found my own Buddhist religion helpful in generating love and compassion, I am convinced that these qualities can be developed by anyone, with or without religion. I further believe that all religions pursue the same goals: those of cultivating goodness and bringing happiness to all human beings. Though the means might appear different, the ends are the same.

TENZIN GYATSO, THE FOURTEENTH
DALAI LAMA OF TIBET (20TH CENTURY)

Mankind is interdependent, and the happiness of each depends upon the happiness of all, and it is this lesson that humanity has to learn today as the first and the last lesson.

HAZRAT INAYAT KHAN (20TH CENTURY)

You learn love by loving – by paying attention and doing what one thereby discovers has to be done.

ALDOUS HUXLEY (20TH CENTURY)

The way is not in the sky. The way is in the heart.

THE DHAMMAPADA (6TH CENTURY BC)

Never in the world does hatred cease by
hatred; hatred ceases by love.

THE BUDDHA (6TH CENTURY BC)

One word frees us of all the weight and pain
of life: that word is love.

SOPHOCLES (5TH CENTURY BC)

Love is all we have, the only way that each
can help the other.

EURIPIDES (5TH CENTURY BC)

If you sit down at set of sun
And count the acts that you have done,
    And, counting, find
One self-denying deed, one word
That eased the heart of him who heard,
    One glance most kind
That fell like sunshine where it went –
Then you may count that day well spent.

But if, through all the livelong day,
You've cheered no heart, by yea or nay –
    If, through it all
You've nothing done that you can trace
That bought the sunshine to one face –
    No act most small
That helped some soul and nothing cost –
Then count that day as worse than lost.

GEORGE ELIOT (19TH CENTURY)

Love makes bitter things sweet; love converts base copper to gold. By love dregs become clear; by love pains become healing. By love the dead are brought to life; by love a king is made a slave.

JALAL AL-DIN RUMI (13TH CENTURY)

Do not waste time bothering whether you 'love' your neighbour; act as if you did. As soon as we do this, we find one of the greatest secrets. When you are behaving as if you love someone, you will presently come to love him.

C. S. LEWIS (20TH CENTURY)

If I can stop one heart from breaking,

I shall not live in vain;

If I can ease one life the aching,

Or cool one pain,

Or help one fainting robin

Unto his rest again,

I shall not live in vain.

EMILY DICKINSON (19TH CENTURY)

Fellowship is heaven, and lack of fellowship is hell; fellowship is life, and lack of fellowship is death; and the deeds that ye do upon the earth, it is for fellowship's sake that ye do them.

WILLIAM MORRIS (19TH CENTURY)

There is no need to go searching for a remedy for the evils of the time. The remedy already exists – it is the gift of one's self to those who have fallen so low that even hope fails them. Open wide your heart.

RENÉ BAZIN (19TH–20TH CENTURY)

The highest wisdom is kindness.

THE TALMUD (4TH CENTURY)

This we know. The Earth does not belong to man; man belongs to the Earth. This we know. All things are connected like blood which unites one family. Whatever befalls the Earth befalls the sons of the Earth. Man did not weave the web of life; he is merely a strand in it. Whatever he does to the web, he does to himself.

CHIEF SEATTLE (19TH CENTURY)

No man is an island entire of itself;

Every man is a piece of the continent, a part of the
   main;

If a clod be washed away by the sea,

Europe is the less, as well as if a promontory were,

As well as if a manor of thy friends

Or of thine own were;

Any man's death diminishes me, because I am
   involved in mankind;

And therefore, never send to know for whom the
   bell tolls;

It tolls for thee.

JOHN DONNE (16TH–17TH CENTURY)

If you can learn a simple trick, you'll get
along a lot better with all kinds of folks. You
never really understand a person until you
consider things from his point of view ... until
you climb into his skin and walk around in it.

HARPER LEE (20TH CENTURY)

We must widen the circle of our love until it
embraces the whole village; the village in
turn must take into its fold the district; the
district the province, and so on till the scope
of our love encompasses the whole world.

M.K. GANDHI (20TH CENTURY)

Man must evolve for all human conflict a
method which rejects revenge, aggression,
and retaliation. The foundation of such a
method is love.

MARTIN LUTHER KING (20TH CENTURY)

This is my commandment, that you love
one another as I have loved you.

JOHN 15:12 (1ST CENTURY)

Do you love your Creator? Then love your
fellow beings first.

THE KORAN (7TH CENTURY)

To those who are good to me I am good. To
those who are not good to me I am good
also. Thus all get to be good.

LAO TZU (4TH CENTURY BC)

But I say unto you, love your enemies.
Bless them that curse you and pray for them
that despitefully use you.

LUKE 6:27 (1ST CENTURY)

All are but parts of one stupendous whole,
Whose body nature is, and God the soul.

ALEXANDER POPE (18TH CENTURY)

Love alone can unite living beings so as to
complete and fulfil them ... for it alone joins
them by what is deepest in themselves. All
we need is to imagine our ability to love
developing until it embraces the totality of
men and of the earth.

PIERRE TEILHARD DE CHARDIN (20TH CENTURY)

There is no path greater than love.
There is no law higher than love.
And there is no goal beyond love.
God and love are identical.

MEHER BABA (20TH CENTURY)

It is only with the heart that one can see rightly.
What is essential is invisible to the eye.

ANTOINE DE SAINT EXUPÉRY (20TH CENTURY)

Love alters not with Time's brief hours and weeks,
But bears it out even to the edge of doom.

WILLIAM SHAKESPEARE (16TH–17TH CENTURY)

There is no difficulty that enough love will
    not conquer,
no disease that enough love will not heal;
no door that enough love will not open;
no gulf that enough love will not bridge;
no wall that enough love will not throw down;
no sin that enough love will not redeem ...
It makes no difference how deeply seated
may be the trouble; how hopeless the outlook;
how muddled the tangle; how great the mistake.
A sufficient realization of love will dissolve it all.
If only you could love enough you would be
    the happiest
and most powerful being in the world.

EMMET FOX (20TH CENTURY)

One word frees us from the weight and pain
    of life; that word is love.

SOPHOCLES (5TH CENTURY)

145

Love is a medicine for the sickness of the world; a prescription often given, too rarely taken.

KARL A. MENNINGER (20TH CENTURY)

You know quite well deep within you, that there is only a single magic, a single power, a single salvation ... and that is called loving.

HERMANN HESSE (20TH CENTURY)

And in a sense love is everything. It is the key to life, and its influences are those that move the world. Live only in the thought of love for all and you will draw love to you from all.

RALPH WALDO TRINE (19TH CENTURY)

The words of Jesus, 'Love one another as I have loved you', must be not only a light to us but a flame that consumes the self in us.

MOTHER TERESA (20TH CENTURY)

Love is something you and I must have. We must have it because our spirit feeds upon it. We must have it because without it we become weak and faint. ... Without it our courage fails. Without love, we can no longer look confidently at the world. We turn inward ... and little by little we destroy ourselves. With it, we are creative. With it, we march tirelessly. With it, and with it alone, we are able to sacrifice for others.

CHIEF DAN GEORGE (20TH CENTURY)

When you come to be sensibly touched, the scales will fall from your eyes; and by the penetrating eyes of love you will discern that which your other eyes will never see.

FRANÇOIS DE LA MOTHE FÉNELON (18TH CENTURY)

Right from the moment of our birth, we are under the care and kindness of our parents. And then later on in our life, when we are oppressed by sickness and become old, we are again dependent on the kindness of others. And since at the beginning and end of our lives, we are so dependent on others' kindness, how can it be in the middle that we neglect kindness towards others?

TENZIN GYATSO, THE FOURTEENTH
DALAI LAMA OF TIBET (20TH CENTURY)

Try to treat with equal love all the people
with whom you have relations. Thus the
abyss between 'myself' and 'yourself' will
be filled in, which is the goal of all religious
worship.

ANANDAMAYI MA NIRMALA SUNDARI DEVI
(20TH CENTURY)

꩜

The soul is made of love and must ever
strive to return to love. Therefore it can
never find rest nor happiness in other
things. It must lose itself in love. By its very
nature it must seek God, who is love.

MECHTHILD OF MAGDEBURG (13TH CENTURY)

꩜

Love seeks no cause beyond itself and no
fruit; it is its own fruit, its own enjoyment.
I love because I love; I love in order that I
may love.

SAINT BERNARD (12TH CENTURY)

The simple fact remains, however, that the stronger and more radiant we are, the more we can serve as a positive influence in the world. The more happiness we bring into the world, the better it is for everyone.

DAN MILLMAN (20TH CENTURY)

Love seeketh not itself to please,
Nor for itself hath any care,
But for another gives its ease,
And builds a Heaven in Hell's despair.

WILLIAM BLAKE (18TH–19TH CENTURY)

Ten

❧

THERE IS A PURPOSE! —
LIFE IS A GREAT OPPORTUNITY

IN TODAY'S WORLD OF FRENETIC ACTIVITY, WITH ITS
emphasis on material success and consumption, it's easy to
lose sight of what life's really about. Status and wealth
clearly don't give meaning to our lives – indeed, there's a
greater chance they will make it less meaningful, as our
newspapers all too frequently testify, with their stories of the
rich and famous who have turned to drink, drugs or suicide.

A sense of meaning and purpose in life is as vital as the
air we breathe, or the food or water necessary to sustain us.
Without meaning, life withers.

We want to feel happy and fulfilled, but this is not
the same as having pleasurable experiences. Rather it's a

question of our souls being nourished. We find meaning through our efforts to achieve something worthwhile, through using our talents, through our relationships – in other words, through becoming fully mature human beings. Ultimately, it's the connection to a larger reality – the whole, the universe, God, Spirit, whatever we call it – which gives meaning and purpose to our lives.

But what about adversity and pain? They seem to serve little purpose, until we understand that they can be a stimulus for spiritual growth and transformation. They are the very means by which we grow as human beings. In coping with difficulties in life, we can often come to appreciate that there is meaning in our suffering. Sadness can open up our hearts and make us more compassionate, while evil provides the opportunity for us to be courageous and to triumph over it. Ultimately, life provides us with the opportunity to learn and acquire wisdom – and there lies serenity.

Only human beings have come to a point
where they no longer know why they exist.
They ... have forgotten the secret
knowledge of their bodies, their senses,
their dreams.

LAME DEER (20TH CENTURY)

The proper function of man is to live, not
to exist.

JACK LONDON (19TH–20TH CENTURY)

The lack of meaning in life is a soul-
sickness whose full extent and full import
our age has not as yet begun to comprehend.

C. G. JUNG (20TH CENTURY)

The great malady of the twentieth century, implicated in all of our troubles and affecting us individually and socially, is 'loss of the soul'. When soul is neglected, it doesn't just go away; it appears symptomatically in obsessions, addictions, violence, and loss of meaning. Our temptation is to isolate these symptoms or to try to eradicate them one by one; but the root problem is that we have lost our wisdom about the soul, even our interest in it.

THOMAS MOORE (20TH CENTURY)

Every soul is created for a certain purpose – the light of that purpose has been kindled in every soul.

SA'DI (13TH CENTURY)

To remain healthy, man must have some
goal, some purpose in life that he can
respect and be proud to work for.

HANS SELYE (20TH CENTURY)

❧

Achieving or experiencing happiness is the
purpose of life.

TENZIN GYATSO, THE FOURTEENTH
DALAI LAMA OF TIBET (20TH CENTURY)

❧

This is our purpose: to make as meaningful
as possible this life that has been bestowed
upon us; to live in such a way that we may
be proud of ourselves; to act in such a way
that some part of us lives on.

OSWALD SPENGLER (20TH CENTURY)

So to conduct one's life as to realize oneself
– this seems to me the highest attainment
possible to a human being.

HENRIK IBSEN (19TH CENTURY)

The greatest use of life is to spend it for
something that will outlast it.

WILLIAM JAMES (19TH CENTURY)

In the lives of many people it is possible to
find a unifying purpose that justifies the
things they do day in, day out – a goal that
like a magnetic field attracts their psychic
energy, a goal upon which all lesser goals
depend ... Without such a purpose, even the
best-ordered consciousness lacks meaning.

MIHALY CSIKSZENTMIHALYI (20TH CENTURY)

Life means to have something definite
to do – a mission to fulfil – and in the
measure in which we avoid setting our life
to something, we make it empty. Human
life, by its very nature, has to be dedicated
to something.

JOSÉ ORTEGA Y GASSET (20TH CENTURY)

What gives meaning to our life is being
connected to something beyond our own
ego. This is an essentially spiritual
experience.

JAMES W. JONES (20TH CENTURY)

God alone is Real, and the goal of life is to
become united with Him through Love.

MEHER BABA (20TH CENTURY)

Again and again the sacred texts tell us that
our life's purpose is to understand and
develop the power of spirit, power that is
vital to our mental and physical well-being.

Caroline Myss (20th century)

If you believe in God, then your search
must be for God; but even if you believe in
nothing, you must still have some conviction
that there is a *meaning* behind the visible
world. You must be determined to seek out
that meaning and understand it.

Shivapuri Baba (20th century)

To return to the root is to find the meaning.
But to pursue appearances is to miss the
source.

SENG-TS'AN (SOSAN) (6TH CENTURY)

Although all men have a common destiny,
each individual must also work out his personal salvation for himself ... In the last
analysis, each is responsible for 'finding
himself'.

THOMAS MERTON (20TH CENTURY)

Existence is a strange bargain. Life owes us
little; we owe it everything. The only true
happiness comes from squandering
ourselves for a purpose.

WILLIAM COWPER (18TH CENTURY)

To bring our will into harmony with the
sacred law is to understand our life purpose.
Why am I here, what are my gifts? Human
life is a great opportunity. Each one has
particular gifts, a unique role in the circle.
Conscious will become manifest as one
dedicates one's gifts for the benefit
of family, clan, nation, all beings.

DHYANI YWAHOO (20TH CENTURY)

He who has a why to live can bear almost
any how.

FRIEDRICH NIETZSCHE (19TH CENTURY)

People say that what we're all seeking, is a
meaning for life. I don't think that's what
we're really seeking. I think that what we're
really seeking is an experience of being
alive, so that our life experiences on the
purely physical plane will have resonances
within our innermost being and reality, so
that we can actually feel the rapture of being
alive.

JOSEPH CAMPBELL (20TH CENTURY)

The oldest wisdom in the world tells us we
can consciously unite with the divine while
in this body; for this man is really born. If he
misses his destiny, Nature is not in a hurry;
she will catch him up some day, and compel
him to fulfil her secret purpose.

SARVEPALLI RADHAKRISHNAN (20TH CENTURY)

There is no use in one person attempting to tell another what the meaning of life is. It involves too intimate an awareness. A major part of the meaning of life is contained in the very discovering of it. It is an ongoing experience of growth that involves a deepening contact with reality. To speak as though it were an objective knowledge, like the date of the war of 1812, misses the point altogether. The meaning of life is indeed objective when it is reached, but the way to it is by a path of subjectivities ... The meaning of life cannot be told; it has to happen to a person.

IRA PROGOFF (20TH CENTURY)

No matter what situation you are in right now, there is a purpose to that situation, and I believe that you are not off the mark. You may not want to stay in a particular situation for long, but a meaningful purpose has brought you to this place. By working with the specific conditions in front of you, you will begin to discover things about yourself that will give you clues to the next step. Your job will be to look, listen, feel, choose, and act.

CAROL ADRIENNE (20TH CENTURY)

We must be able to still ourselves, to tune our spirit to the universal consciousness in order to know the purpose of our life. And once we know the purpose, the best thing is to pursue it in spite of all difficulties. Nothing should discourage us, nothing should keep us back once we know that this is the purpose of our life.

HAZRAT INAYAT KHAN (20TH CENTURY)

Eleven

❧

WORK TO LIVE —
TRUE WORK IS SERVICE

AS WE LOOK TOWARDS THE FUTURE WE MIGHT WANT TO rethink our attitude towards work. Work is an essential part of life – we work to live, though increasingly in the Western world it sometimes seems as if we live to work. The world of work has changed beyond all recognition – with long hours, pressure to perform and tight deadlines. Delivering ever-increasing profits is questionable anyway, but the drive to do so often results in a lifestyle that is unbalanced, unhealthy and unfulfilling.

Work should be more than a means to make money and support ourselves, or to achieve a goal. There is no reason why it shouldn't do both, but if satisfaction and fulfilment are not to elude us, and if we want our lives to be more sane, then work has to have meaning. We need to use our skills and talents, putting our energy into something we can take pride in and which is of service to others. If we are not using our skills in a way that imbues our lives with meaning, then we should endeavour to find other means to use them. In the New Testament, in the Parable of the Talents, Jesus makes very clear how important it is to use our skills for the benefit of others, and not to let them go to waste.

Right livelihood is one of the eight key concepts of the path of Buddhism and speaks of making one's life work helpful to other people. Exploiting others, unethical investment, using up the earth's resources without replacing them – all these are issues which are becoming increasingly important for the future.

We can't be personally responsible for everything that is wrong in the world, but we can keep our own house in order, and do what we can to serve. This may not necessarily mean feeding the hungry and homeless or working with the sick and dying – each of us can make a meaningful contribution through what we do in our daily lives – through the way we behave in the workplace, through our use of our free time, through how we relate to everyone with whom we come into contact. The more we give of ourselves, the more we get back, and in the process we become more at peace with ourselves.

We cannot hope to build a better world without improving the individual. Towards this end, each of us must work towards his own highest development, accepting at the same time his share of responsibility in the general life of humanity – our particular duty being to help those to whom we feel we can be most useful.

MARIE CURIE (19TH–20TH CENTURY)

We cannot live only for ourselves. A thousand fibers connect us with our fellow men; and among those fibers, as sympathetic threads, our actions run as causes, and they come back to us as effects.

HERMAN MELVILLE (19TH CENTURY)

It is high time the ideal of success should be replaced with the ideal of service.

ALBERT EINSTEIN (19TH–20TH CENTURY)

One cannot pursue one's own highest good without at the same time necessarily promoting the good of others. A life based on narrow self-interest cannot be esteemed by any honourable measurement. Seeking the very best in ourselves means actively caring for the welfare of other human beings. Our human contact is not with the few people with whom our affairs are most immediately intertwined, nor to the prominent, rich, or well-educated, but to all our human brethren.

View yourself as a citizen of a worldwide community and act accordingly.

EPICTETUS (1ST–2ND CENTURY)

Our age has its own particular mission ... the creation of a civilization founded upon the spiritual nature of work.

SIMONE WEIL (20TH CENTURY)

We all have, without exception, a very deep longing to give – to give to the earth, to give to others, to give to society, to work, to love, to care for this earth. That's true for every human being. And even the ones who don't find it, it's because it has been squashed or somehow suppressed in some brutal way in their life. But it's there to be discovered. We all long for that.

And there's a tremendous sorrow for a human being who doesn't find a way to give. One of the worst of human sufferings is not to find a way to love, or a place to work and give your heart and being.

JACK KORNFIELD (20TH CENTURY)

It is important to work for future generations, for our descendants. We must be proud to do something, even though people do not usually know its value.

SHUNRYU SUZUKI ROSHI (20TH CENTURY)

If a person works only for himself he can perhaps be a famous scholar, a great wise man, a distinguished poet, but never a complete, genuinely great man. History calls those the greatest ... who ennobled themselves by working for the universal. Experience praises as the most happy the one who made the most people happy.

KARL MARX (19TH CENTURY)

Man becomes great exactly in the degree to which he works for the welfare of his fellow man.

M.K. GANDHI (20TH CENTURY)

The noblest service comes from nameless hands,
And the best servant does his work unseen.

OLIVER WENDELL HOLMES (19TH CENTURY)

The only ones among you who will be really
happy are those who will have sought and
found how to serve.

ALBERT SCHWEITZER (20TH CENTURY)

I slept and dreamt that life was joy
I awoke and saw that life was service
I acted and behold, service was joy.

RABINDRANATH TAGORE (19TH–20TH CENTURY)

It is within my power either to serve God, or
not to serve Him. Serving Him, I add to my
own good and the good of the whole world.
Not serving Him, I forfeit my own good and
deprive the world of that good, which was
in my power to create.

LEO TOLSTOY (19TH CENTURY)

It is one of the most beautiful
compensations of this life that no man can
sincerely try to help another without helping
himself.

RALPH WALDO EMERSON (19TH CENTURY)

As we live we are transmitters of life and when we fail to transmit life, life fails to flow through us ... And if, as we work, we can transmit life into our work, still more life rushes in to compensate, to be ready and we ripple with life through the days ...

Give and it shall be given unto you is still the truth about life. But giving life is not so easy. It doesn't mean handing it out to some mean fool or letting the living dead eat you up. ... It means kindling the life force where it was not, even if it's only in the whiteness of a washed pocket handkerchief.

D. H. LAWRENCE (20TH CENTURY)

And what is it to work with love?

It is to weave the cloth with threads drawn from
your heart, even as if your beloved were to
wear that cloth.

It is to build a house with affection, even as if your
beloved were to dwell in that house.

It is to sow seeds with tenderness and reap the
harvest with joy, even as if your beloved were
to eat the fruit.

It is to charge all things you fashion with a breath
of your own spirit ...

KAHLIL GIBRAN (20TH CENTURY)

Your work is to discover your work and then
with all your heart give yourself to it.

THE BUDDHA (6TH CENTURY BC)

Teach us, good Lord,

to serve you as you deserve;

to give and not to count the cost,

to fight and not to heed the wounds,

to toil and not to seek for rest,

to labour and not to ask for any reward,

save that of knowing that we do your will;

through Jesus Christ our Lord. Amen.

IGNATIUS LOYOLA (16TH CENTURY)

Each one of you has received a special
grace, so, like stewards responsible for all
these different graces of God, put yourselves
at the service of others. If you are a speaker,
speak in words that seem to come from God;
if you are a helper, help as though every
action was done at God's orders; so that in
everything God may receive the glory.

1 PETER 4:10–11 (1ST CENTURY)

Make us worthy, Lord,

to serve our fellow men throughout the world,

who live and die in poverty and hunger.

Give them by our hands

this day their daily bread,

and by our understanding love

give peace and joy.

POPE PAUL VI (20TH CENTURY)

Teach me, my God and King

In all things thee to see;

And what I do in anything

To do it for thee!

A servant with this clause

Makes drudgery divine;

Who sweeps a room, as for thy laws,

Makes that and the action fine.

GEORGE HERBERT (17TH CENTURY)

Each small task of everyday life is part of
the total harmony of the universe.

SAINT THÉRÈSE OF LISIEUX (19TH CENTURY)

A hundred times every day I remind myself
that my inner and outer life depends on the
labors of other men, living and dead, and
that I must exert myself in order to give in
the measure as I have received and am still
receiving.

ALBERT EINSTEIN (19TH–20TH CENTURY)

Lives of great men remind us
We can make our lives sublime,
And, departing, leave behind us
Footprints on the sands of time.

HENRY WADSWORTH LONGFELLOW (19TH CENTURY)

The wise devote themselves to the welfare
of all, for they see themselves in all.

UPANISHADS (6TH CENTURY BC)

To leave the world a little bit better,
whether by a healthy child, a garden patch,
or a redeemed social condition;
To know that even one life has breathed easier
because you have lived:
This is to have succeeded.

THOMAS STANLEY (17TH CENTURY)

The highest reward for a person's toil is not
what they get for it but what they become
by it.

JOHN RUSKIN (19TH CENTURY)

I sought my soul, but my soul I could not see.

I sought my God, but my God eluded me.

I sought my brother and I found all three.

ANONYMOUS

For I was hungry and you gave Me meat;

I was thirsty and you gave Me drink;

I was a stranger and you took Me in.

I was naked and you clothed Me;

I was sick and you visited Me.

I was in prison and you came to Me.

MATTHEW 25:35–6 (1ST CENTURY)

There are no passengers on Spaceship
Earth. Everybody's crew.

MARSHALL McLUHAN (20TH CENTURY)

This is the true joy in life, the being used for a purpose recognized by yourself as a mighty one; the being thoroughly worn out before you are thrown on the scrap heap; the being a force of nature instead of a feverish selfish little clod of ailments and grievances complaining that the world will not devote itself to making you happy.

I am of the opinion that my life belongs to the whole community and as long as I live it is my privilege to do for it whatever I can. I want to be thoroughly used up when I die. For the harder I work the more I live. I rejoice in life for its own sake. Life is no brief candle to me. It's a sort of splendid torch which I've got to hold up for the moment and I want to make it burn as brightly as possible before handing it on to future generations.

GEORGE BERNARD SHAW (19TH–20TH CENTURY)

O God! make me busy with thee, that they
may not make me busy with them.

RABI'A AL ADAWIYYA (8TH CENTURY)

Whatever you do, make it an offering to me
– the food you eat, the sacrifices you make,
the help you give, even your suffering.

BHAGAVAD GITA (2ND CENTURY BC)

The time of business does not with me dif-
fer from the time of prayer, and in the noise
and clatter of my kitchen, while several
persons are at the same time calling for
different things, I possess God in as great
tranquillity as if I were upon my knees at
the blessed sacrament.

BROTHER LAWRENCE (17TH CENTURY)

This and this alone
Is true religion –
To serve thy brethren:

This is sin above all other sin,
To harm thy brethren:

In such a faith is happiness,
In lack of it is misery and pain:

Blessed is he who swerveth not aside
From this strait path:
Blessed is he whose life is lived
Thus ceaselessly in serving God.

By bearing others' burdens,
And so alone,
Is life, true life, to be attained:

Nothing is hard to him who, casting self aside,
Thinks only this –
How may I serve my fellow-men.

TULSIDAS (16–17TH CENTURY)
(TRANSLATED FROM THE SANSKRIT BY M.K. GANDHI)

Do all the good you can,

By all the means you can,

In all the ways you can,

In all the places you can,

At all the times you can,

To all the people you can,

As long as ever you can.

JOHN WESLEY (18TH CENTURY)

Every kind of work can be a pleasure. Even simple household tasks can be an opportunity to exercise and expand our caring, our effectiveness, our responsiveness.

As we respond with caring and vision to all work, we develop our capacity to respond fully to all of life. Every action generates the energy which can be shared with others. These qualities of caring and responsiveness are the greatest gift we can offer.

TARTHANG TULKU (20TH CENTURY)

Life is a field and you are born to cultivate it.
... All that your soul yearns after and all you
need is to be got from the field, if you know
how to cultivate it and how to reap the fruit.

KABIR (15TH CENTURY)

Strange as it may seem, life becomes serene
and enjoyable precisely when selfish
pleasures and personal success are no longer
the guiding goals.

MIHALY CSIKSZENTMIHALYI (20TH CENTURY)

Make the decision to serve wherever you go
and to whomever you see. As long as you are
serving, you will be receiving. The more
you serve, the more confidence you will gain
in the miraculous effects of this principle
of life.

GREG ANDERSON (20TH CENTURY)

Twelve

~

LIVE SIMPLY —
AND BECOME 'TIME-RICH'
INSTEAD OF 'TIME-SQUEEZED'

IN A WORLD THAT HAS BECOME EVER MORE COMPLEX, it's a real challenge to live simply. Work and the consumer culture are seductive, but there comes a point when we realize that we've sacrificed too much. We suddenly see that life has become too complicated, and we're exhausted by it all. Material improvements in our lives often mean that we've lost contact with the simple things of life. Struggling to survive in an affluent society means that we've no time to enjoy our achievements, inadequate time for our relation-ships, no time for ourselves. Simple pleasures bring greater satisfaction than material possessions, simple pastimes don't cost the earth, simple food is likely to keep us healthier, and when we live simply, we're much less likely to feel stressed and get sick.

The life of multiplicity that we live tends to result in fragmentation and alienation, not balance, which is what we long for in our lives. A life of simplicity, where we cut back on some of the meaningless distractions, and slow down, re-evaluating our lives and what we need, enables us to live more creatively, and that means that we will feel more fulfilled, and there will be more joy. In cramming less into our lives we experience more. We're 'time-rich' instead of 'time-squeezed'!

The problem is ... how to remain whole in
the midst of the distractions of life; how to
remain balanced, no matter what centrifugal
forces tend to pull one off center; how to
remain strong, no matter what shocks come
in at the periphery and tend to crack the
hub of the wheel.

ANNE MORROW LINDBERGH (20TH CENTURY)

Teach us to delight in simple things.

RUDYARD KIPLING (19TH–20TH CENTURY)

We are not rich by what we possess
But rather by what we can do without.

IMMANUEL KANT (18TH CENTURY)

Simplicity allows the senses to rest from
stimulation.

GUNILLA NORRIS (20TH CENTURY)

Simplicity, simplicity, simplicity! I say let your
affairs be as two or three, and not a hundred or
a thousand; instead of a million count half a
dozen ... In the midst of this chopping sea of
civilized life, such are the clouds and storms
and quicksands and the thousand-and-one
items to be allowed for, that a man has to live,
if he would not founder and go to the bottom
and not make his part at all, by dead reckoning,
and he must be a great calculator indeed who
succeeds. Simplify, simplify.

HENRY DAVID THOREAU (19TH CENTURY)

'Tis a gift to be simple, 'Tis a gift to be free.

SHAKER HYMN (18TH CENTURY)

There is no greatness where there is not
simplicity, goodness and truth.

LEO TOLSTOY (19TH CENTURY)

To live content with small means,
to seek elegance rather than luxury,
and refinement rather than fashion,
to be worthy, not respectable, and wealthy, not rich,
to study hard, think quietly, talk gently, act frankly,
to listen to stars and birds, babes and sages, with
    open heart,
to bear all cheerfully,
do all bravely,
await occasions,
hurry never –
in a word, to let the spiritual, unbidden and
    unconscious,
grow up through the common.
This is to be my symphony.

WILLIAM ELLERY CHANNING (19TH CENTURY)

I will arise and go now, and go to Innisfree,
And a small cabin build there, of clay and wattles
     made:
Nine bean-rows will I have there, a hive for the
     honey-bee,
And live alone in the bee-land glade.

And I shall have some peace there, for peace
     comes dropping slow,
Dropping from the veils of the morning to where
     the cricket sings;
There midnight's all a glimmer, and noon a purple
     glow,
And evening full of the linnet's wings.

I will arise and go now, for always night and day
I hear lake water lapping with low sounds by the
     shore;
While I stand on the roadway, or on the pavements
     grey,
I hear it in the deep heart's core.

W. B. YEATS (19TH–20TH CENTURY)

Leave off that excessive desire of knowing;

therein is found much distraction.

There are many things the knowledge of which

is of little or no profit to the soul.

THOMAS À KEMPIS (15TH CENTURY)

Manifest plainness,

Embrace simplicity,

Reduce selfishness,

Have few desires.

LAO TZU (4TH CENTURY BC)

Too lazy to be ambitious,

I let the world take care of itself.

Ten days worth of rice in my bag;

a bundle of twigs by the fireplace.

Why chatter about delusion and enlightenment?

Learning to listen to the night rain on my roof,

I sit comfortably, with both legs stretched out.

RYOKAN (18TH–19TH CENTURY)
TRANSLATED BY STEPHEN MITCHELL

The great lesson ... is that the sacred is *in*
the ordinary, that it is to be found in one's
daily life, in one's neighbors, friends, and
family, in one's back yard ...

ABRAHAM MASLOW (20TH CENTURY)

Besides the noble art of getting things done,
there is the noble art of leaving things undone.
The wisdom of life consists
in the elimination of nonessentials.

LIN YUTANG (20TH CENTURY)

I am convinced, both by faith and
experience, that to maintain one's self on
the earth is not a hardship but a pastime – if
we live simply and wisely.

HENRY DAVID THOREAU (19TH CENTURY)

Consciously cultivating simplicity in our lives and within ourselves is one of the most direct means of achieving well-being, peace and harmony ... If we deeply value a calmer, more open and sensitive mind and heart it may involve some simplification of our lives. Cultivating simplicity has profound implications not only for the quality of our own well-being, but equally for the quality of our world. In voluntary or conscious simplicity as a way of life we are taking only that which we need ...

CHRISTINA FELDMAN (20TH CENTURY)

One cannot collect all the beautiful shells on the beach. One can collect only a few, and they are more beautiful if they are few. One moon shell is more impressive than three. There is only one moon in the sky. One double-sunrise is an event; six are a succession, like a week of school-days. Gradually one discards and keeps just the perfect specimen; not necessarily a rare shell, but a perfect one of its kind. One sets it apart by itself, ringed around by space – like an island.

For it is only framed in space that beauty blooms. Only in space are events and objects and people unique and significant – and therefore beautiful ...

ANNE MORROW LINDBERGH (20TH CENTURY)

Simply seek happiness, and you are not likely to find it. Seek to create and love without regard to your happiness, and you will likely be happy much of the time. Seeking joy in and of itself will not bring it to you. Do the work of creating community, and you will obtain it – although never exactly according to your schedule. Joy is an uncapturable yet utterly predictable side effect of genuine community.

M. Scott Peck (20th century)

My daily affairs are quite ordinary;
but I'm in total harmony with them.
I don't hold on to anything, don't reject anything;
nowhere an obstacle or conflict.
Who cares about wealth and honor?
Even the poorest thing shines.
My miraculous power and spiritual activity:
drawing water and carrying wood.

Layman P'ang (8th century)
translated by Stephen Mitchell

Acknowledgements and Further Reading

The editor would like to thank the following authors and publishers for permission to reprint material from their books:

Adrienne, Carol, *The Purpose of Your Life*, Thorsons, 1998.

Anderson, Greg, *Living Life on Purpose: A Guide to Creating a Life of Success and Significance*, HarperSanFrancisco, 1997.

Bassett, E. (ed.), *Love is my Meaning*, Darton, Longman & Todd, 1973.

Campbell, Joseph, with Moyers, Bill, *The Power of Myth*, Doubleday, 1988.

Chief Dan George, 'My Heart Soars', from *Saanichtoni*, Hancock House Publishers, 1974.

Cousineau, Phil (ed.), *Soul: An Archaeology: Readings from Socrates to Ray Charles*, HarperSanFrancisco, 1994.

Csikszentmihalyi, Mihaly, *The Evolving Self*, HarperPerennial, 1994.

e.e. cummings (edited by George J. Firmage), *Complete Poems 1904–62*, W.W. Norton.

Dillard Annie, *Holy the Firm*, HarperCollins, NY, 1977.

Dillard, Annie, *Pilgrim at Tinker Creek*, Picador, 1976.

Epictetus (a new interpretation by Sharon Lebell), *A Manual for Living*, HarperSanFrancisco, 1994.

Foundation for Inner Peace, *A Course in Miracles*, Tiburon, California, 1975.

Fry, Christopher, *A Sleep of Prisoners*, OUP © 1951, 1959.

Gibran, Kahlil, *The Prophet* (copyright 1923, Kahlil Gibran; renewal copyright, 1951), Knopf, New York, Random House, 1926.

Guillevic, 'When Each Day is Sacred', from *Selected Poems*, translated by Denise Levertov © 1969, New Directions Publishing.

Hay, Louise, *You Can Heal Your Life*, Eden Grove Edition, 1988.

Hazrat Inayat Khan, *Gayan Vadan Nirtan*, Sufi Order Publications, Lebanon Springs, New York, 1980.

Houston, Jean, *The Possible Human: A Course in Enhancing*

Your Physical, Mental and Creative Abilities, J. P. Tarcher, Los Angeles, 1982.

Jones, James W., *In The Middle Of This Road We Call Our Life: Connecting with Your Heart's Desires*, HarperSanFrancisco, 1995 and Thorsons, 1995.

Jampolsky, Gerald G., *Love is Letting Go of Fear*, Celestial Arts, Millbrae, California, 1979.

Kabat-Zinn, Jon, *Wherever You Go There You Are*, Hyperion, 1995.

Keay, Kathy, 'In The Garden' from *Laughter, Silence and Shouting: An Anthology of Women's Prayers*, HarperCollins, 1994.

Kornfield, Jack and Feldman, Christina, *Soul Food: Stories to Nourish the Spirit and the Heart*, HarperSanFrancisco, 1996.

Lao Tzu (translated by Stephen Mitchell), *Tao Te Ching*, HarperCollinsPublishers, NY, 1988.

Lindbergh, Anne Morrow, *Gifts from the Sea*, Pantheon Books, 1975.

Marciniak, Barbara, *Bringers of the Dawn: Teachings from the Pleiadiam*, Bear & Co, Santa Fe, New Mexico, 1992.

Mitchell, Stephen (trans.), *Tao Te Ching by Lao-Tzu*, Harper & Row, 1988.

Mitchell, Stephen (ed.) *The Enlightened Heart: An Anthology of Sacred Poetry*, Harper & Row, 1989.

Moore, Thomas, *Care of the Soul: How to Add Depth and Meaning to Your Everyday Life*, HarperCollins, New York, 1992.

Myss, Caroline, *Anatomy of the Spirit*, Bantam Books, 1997.

Norris, Gunilla, *Sharing Silence: Meditation Practice and Mindful Living*, Bell Tower, New York, 1992.

P'Ang, Layman (translated by Stephen Mitchell), *The Enlightened Heart*, HarperCollinsPublishers, NY, 1989.

Pearson, Carol S., *Awakening the Heroes Within: Twelve Archetypes to Help Us Find Ourselves and Transform Our World*, HarperSanFrancisco, 1991.

Pound, Ezra, *Collected Shorter Poems*, Faber & Faber, 1968.

Rilke, Rainer Maria (translated by Anita Barrows and Joanne May), *The Book of Hours*, Riverhead Books.

Rinpoche, Sogyal, *Tibetan Book of Living and Dying*, Rider, 1993.

Ryokan (translated by Stephen Mitchell), *The Enlightened Heart*, HarperCollinsPublishers, NY, 1989.

Scott Peck, M., *The Road Less Travelled: A New Psychology of Love, Traditional Values and Spiritual Growth*, Hutchinson, 1978.

Sondheim, Stephen, *Into the Woods*, IMP.

The Dalai Lama, *The Power of Compassion*, Thorsons 1995.

Thoreau, Henry D. (edited by J. Lynden Stanley), *Walden*, Princeton University Press, 1971.

Toms, Justine Willis and Toms, Michael, *True Work*, Bell Tower, 1999.

Trine, Ralph Waldo, *In Tune with the Infinite*, Thorsons, 1991 (first published by G. Bell & Son Ltd, 1899).

Vaughan, Frances E., *Awakening Intuition*, Anchor Press, Doubleday, New York, 1979.

Woodman, Marion, *Coming Home to Myself*, Berkeley, Conari Press, 1998.

Yancey, Philip, *Where is God When It Hurts?* Marshall Pickering, London, 1990.

Yeats, W. B., 'The Lake Isle of Innisfree', from *Selected Poems*, Macmillan, 1982.

Every effort has been made to trace rights holders and to clear reprint permissions. If any acknowledgements have been omitted, or any rights overlooked, we would like to express our regret and request forgiveness. If notified, the publishers will be pleased to rectify any omissions in future editions.